'I thought we had an appointment to meet at six, but since it is now almost eight you appear to have broken it. Shockingly bad manners, Sara. Especially for a future queen of the desert.'

'I'm not going to be a queen of the desert. I have no intention of getting married. Not to Murat and not to anyone! So why waste everybody's time by turning up? Go back to the Sultan and tell him to forget the whole idea.'

Suleiman heard the determination in her voice and felt an unwilling flare of admiration for her unashamed—and very stupid—defiance. Such open insubordination was unheard of in a woman from the desert lands, and it was rather magnificent to observe her spirited rebellion.

He pulled off his dripping coat and hung it on a peg.

She glared at him. 'I don't remember asking you to take your coat off!'

'I don't require your permission.'

'You are impossible!' she hissed.

THE DESERT MEN OF QURHAH

Their destiny is the desert!

The heat of the desert is nothing compared to the passion that burns between the pages of this stunning new trilogy by Sharon Kendrick!

Defiant in the Desert
December 2013

Oil baron Suleiman Al abd Aziz has been sent to retrieve the Sultan of Qurhah's reluctant fiancé— a woman who's utterly forbidden, but is determined to escape the confines of her engagement…by seducing him!

And coming soon…

The Princess of Qurhah's story

The Princess of Qurhah has always wanted something different from her life. So when sexy advertising magnate Gabe Steele arrives to work for her brother, Leila convinces Gabe to give her a job… but that's not the only thing to cause a royal scandal!

The Sultan of Qurhah's story

The Sultan of Qurhah is facing a scandal of epic proportions. His fiancé has run off, leaving him with a space in his king-sized bed. A space once occupied by his mistress—Carly Conner. And now he wants her back—at any price!

DEFIANT IN THE DESERT

BY
SHARON KENDRICK

First published in Great Britain 2013
by Mills & Boon, an imprint of Harlequin (UK) Limited,
Harlequin (UK) Limited, Eton House, 18-24 Paradise Road,
Richmond, Surrey TW9 1SR

© Sharon Kendrick 2013

ISBN: 978 0 263 23589 0

Sharon Kendrick started storytelling at the age of eleven, and has never really stopped. She likes to write fast-paced, feel-good romances with heroes who are so sexy they'll make your toes curl!

Born in west London, she now lives in the beautiful city of Winchester—where she can see the cathedral from her window (but only if she stands on tiptoe). She has two children, Celia and Patrick, and her passions include music, books, cooking and eating—and drifting off into wonderful daydreams while she works out new plots!

Recent titles by the same author:

THE GREEK'S MARRIAGE BARGAIN
A SCANDAL, A SECRET, A BABY
BACK IN THE HEADLINES
  (Scandal in the Spotlight)
A TAINTED BEAUTY

To Peter O'Brien—the intrepid Irishman—who taught me some of the mysteries and miracles of desert life.

CHAPTER ONE

'THERE'S A MAN downstairs in Reception who says he wants to see you.'

'Who is it?' questioned Sara, not bothering to lift her head from the drawing which was currently engrossing her.

'He wouldn't say.'

At this Sara did look up to find Alice, the office runner, staring at her with an odd sort of expression. Alice was young and very enthusiastic, but right now she looked almost *transported*. Her face was tight with excitement and disbelief—as if Santa Claus himself had arrived early with a full contingent of reindeer.

'It's Christmas Eve afternoon,' said Sara, glancing out of the window at the dark grey sky and wincing. No snow, unfortunately. Only a few heavy raindrops spattering against the glass. Pity. Snow might have helped boost her mood—to help shift off the inevitable feeling of *not quite fitting in* which always descended on her at this time of year. She never found it easy to enjoy Christmas—which was one of the main reasons why she tended to ignore the festival until it had gone away.

She pushed a smile to the corners of her mouth, trying to pick up on Alice's happy pre-holiday mood. 'And very soon I'm going to be packing up and going home. If it's a salesman, I'm not interested and if it's anyone else, then tell them to go away and make an appointment to see me in the new year.'

'He says he's not going anywhere,' said Alice and then paused dramatically. 'Until he's seen you.'

Sara put her purple felt-tip pen down with fingers which had annoyingly started to tremble, telling herself not to be so stupid. Telling herself that she was perfectly safe here, in this bright, open-plan office of the highly successful advertising agency where she worked. That there was no reason for this dark feeling of foreboding which had started whispering over her skin.

But of course, there was...

'What do you mean—he's not going anywhere?' she demanded, trying to keep her voice from rising with panic. 'What exactly did he say?'

'That he wants to see you,' repeated Alice and now she made another face which Sara had never seen before. 'And that he craves just a few minutes of your time.'

Craves.

It was a word which jarred like an ice cream eaten on a winter day. No modern Englishman would ever have used a word like that. Sara felt the cold clamp of fear tightening around her heart, like an iron band.

'What...what does he look like?' she asked, her voice a croaky-sounding husk.

Alice played with the pendant which was dangling from her neck in an unconscious display of sexual awareness. 'He's...well, he's pretty unbelievable, if you must know. Not just because of the way he's built—though he must work out practically non-stop to get a body like *that*—but more...more...' Her voice tailed off. 'Well, it's his eyes really.'

'What about his eyes?' barked Sara, feeling her pulse begin to rocket.

'They were like...black. But like, *really* black. Like the sky when there's no moon or stars. Like—'

'Alice,' cut in Sara, desperately trying to inject a note of normality into the girl's uncharacteristically gushing description. Because at that stage she was still trying to fool herself into thinking that it wasn't happening. That it might all be some terrible mistake. A simple mix-up. Anything, but the one thing she most feared. 'Tell him—'

'Why don't you tell me yourself, Sara?'

A cold, accented voice cut through her words and Sara whirled round to see a man standing in the doorway of the office. Shock, pain and desire washed over her in rapid succession. She hadn't seen him for five long years and for a moment she almost didn't recognise him. He had always been dark and utterly gorgeous, gifted with a face and a mind which had captured her heart so completely. But now...

Now...

Her heart pounded.

Something about him had changed.

His dark head was bare and he wore a custom-made

suit instead of his usual robes. The charcoal jacket defined his honed torso just as well as any folds of flowing silk and the immaculately cut trousers emphasised the endless length of his powerful thighs. He had always carried the cachet which came from being the Sultan of Qurhah's closest advisor, but now his natural air of authority seemed to be underpinned with a steely layer Sara had never seen before. And suddenly she recognised it for what it was.

Power.

It seemed to crackle from every pore of his body. To pervade the serene office environment like high-voltage electricity. It made her wary—warier than she felt already, with her heart beating so fast it felt as if it might burst right out of her chest.

'Suleiman,' she said, her voice unsteady and a little unsure. 'What are you doing here?'

He smiled, but it was the coldest smile she had ever seen. Even colder than the one which he had iced into her the last time they'd been together. When he had torn himself away from her passionate embrace and looked down at her as if she was the lowest of the low.

'I think you can probably work that one out for yourself, can't you, Sara?'

He stepped into the office, his clever black eyes narrowing.

'You are an intelligent woman, if a somewhat misguided one,' he continued. 'You have been ignoring repeated requests from the Sultan to return to Qurhah to become his wife. Haven't you?'

'And if I have?'

He looked at her, but there was nothing but indifference in his eyes and, stupidly, that hurt.

'If you have, then you have been behaving like a fool.'

His phrase was coated with an implicit threat which made her skin turn to ice and Sara heard Alice gasp. She turned her head slightly, expecting to see horror on the face of the trendy office runner, with her pink-streaked hair and bottom-hugging skirt. Because it wasn't cool for men to talk that way, was it? But she saw nothing like horror there. Instead, the bohemian youngster was staring at Suleiman with a look of rapt adoration.

Sara swallowed. Cool obviously flew straight out of the window when you had a towering black-haired male standing in your office just oozing testosterone. Why wouldn't Alice acknowledge the presence of a man unlike any other she had probably met? Despite all the attractive hunks who worked in Gabe Steel's advertising empire—didn't Suleiman Abd al-Aziz stand out like a spot of black oil on a white linen dress? Didn't he redefine the very concept of masculinity and make it a hundred times more meaningful?

For her, he had always had the ability to make every other man fade into insignificance—even royal princes and sultans—but now something about him had changed. There was an indefinable quality about him. Something *dangerous*.

Gone was the affection with which he always used to regard her. The man who had drifted in and out of her childhood and taught her to ride seemed to have been replaced by someone else. The black eyes were flat and cold; his lips unsmiling. It wasn't exactly *hatred* she could see on his face—for his expression implied that she wasn't worthy of an emotion as strong as hate. It was more as if she was a *hindrance*. As if he was here under sufferance, in the very last place he wanted to be.

And she had only herself to blame. She knew that. If she hadn't flung herself at him. If she hadn't allowed him to kiss her and then silently invited him to do so much more than that. To...

She tried a smile, though she wasn't sure how convincing a smile it was. She had done everything in her power to forget about Suleiman and the way he'd made her feel, but wasn't it funny how just one glimpse of him could stir up all those familiar emotions? Suddenly her heart was turning over with that painful clench of feeling she'd once thought was love. She could feel the sink of her stomach as she was reminded that he could never be hers.

Well, he would never know that. He wouldn't ever guess that he could still make her feel this way. She wasn't going to give him the chance to humiliate her and reject her. Not again.

'Nice of you to drop in so unexpectedly, Suleiman,' she said, her voice as airy as she could manage. 'But I'm afraid I'm pretty busy at the moment. It *is* Christmas Eve, you know.'

'But you don't celebrate Christmas, Sara. Or at least, I wasn't aware that you did. Have you really changed so much that you have adopted, wholesale, the values of the West?'

He was looking around the large, open-plan office with an expression of distaste curving his carved lips which he didn't bother to hide. His flat black eyes were registering the garish tinsel which was looped over posters depicting some of the company's many successful advertising campaigns. His gaze rested briefly on the old-fashioned fir tree, complete with flashing lights and a glittering star at the top, which had been erected as a kind of passé tribute to Christmases past. His expression darkened.

Sara put her fingers in her lap, horribly aware that they were trembling, and it suddenly became terribly important that he shouldn't see that, either. She didn't want him to think she was scared, even if that moment she was feeling something very close to scared. And she couldn't quite work out what she was afraid of—her, or him.

'Look, I really am *very* busy,' she said. 'And Alice doesn't want to hear—'

'Alice doesn't have to hear anything because she is about to leave us alone to continue this conversation in private,' he said instantly. Turning towards the office junior, he produced a slow smile, like a magician producing a rabbit from a hat. 'Aren't you, Alice?'

Sara watched, unwillingly fascinated as Alice almost melted under the impact of his smile. She even—and Sara had never witnessed this happen before—she even *blushed*. In a single moment, the streetwise girl from London had been transformed into a gushing stereotype from another age. Any minute now and she might actually *swoon*.

'Of course.' Alice fluttered her eyelashes in a way which was also new. 'Though I could get you a cup of coffee first if you like?'

'I am not in the mood for coffee,' said Suleiman and Sara wondered how he managed to make his refusal sound like he was talking about sex. Or was that just her projecting yet more stupid fantasies about him?

He was smiling at the runner and she was smiling right back. 'Even though I imagine that yours would be excellent coffee,' he purred.

'Oh, for heaven's sake! Alice buys coffee from the deli next door,' snapped Sara. 'She wasn't planning on travelling to Brazil and bringing back the beans herself!'

'Then that is Brazil's loss,' murmured Suleiman.

Sara could have screamed at the cheesy line which had the office runner beaming from ear to ear. 'That will be all, thanks, Alice,' she said sharply. 'You can go home now. And have…have a happy Christmas.'

'Thanks,' said Alice, clearly reluctant to leave. 'I'll see you in the new year. Happy Christmas!'

There was complete silence for a moment while they watched the girl gather up her oversized bag, which was crammed with one of the large and expensive presents which had been handed out earlier by Gabe Steel, their boss. Or rather, by his office manager. But it was only after her footsteps had echoed down the corridor towards the lift that Suleiman turned to Sara, his black eyes hard and mocking.

'Quite the little executive these days, aren't you, Sara?'

Sara swallowed. She hated the way he said her name. Or rather, she hated the effect it had on her. The way it made her want to expel a long and shuddering breath and to snake her tongue over lips which had suddenly grown dry. It reminded her too much of the time he had kissed her. When he had overstepped the mark and done the one thing which had been forbidden to him. And to her.

The memory came back as vivid and as real as if it had happened only yesterday. It had been on the night of her brother's coronation—when Haroun had been crowned King of Dhi'ban, a day which many had thought would never come because of the volatile relations between the desert states. All the dignitaries from the neighbouring countries had attended the ceremony—including the infamous Sultan of nearby Qurhah, along with his chief emissary, Suleiman.

Sara remembered being cool and almost non-committal towards the Sultan, to whom she was betrothed. But who could blame her? Her hand in marriage had been the price paid for a financial bail-out for her country. In essence, she had been sold by her father like a piece of human merchandise!

That night she had barely made eye contact with the powerful Sultan who had seemed so forbidding, but her careless attitude seemed to amuse rather than to irritate the potentate. And anyway, he had spent most of the time locked away in meetings with all the other sultans and sheikhs.

But Sara had been eager to be reunited with the Sultan's emissary. She had been filled with pleasure at the thought of seeing Suleiman again, after six long years away at an English boarding school. Suleiman, who had taught her to ride and made her laugh during those two long summers when the Sultan had been negotiating with her father about a financial bail-out. Two summers which had occupied a special place in her heart ever since, even though on that final summer—her marital fate had been sealed.

During the coronation fireworks, she had somehow managed to manoeuvre herself into a position to watch them with Suleiman by her side. The crowds had been so huge that nobody had noticed them standing together and Sara was thrilled just to be in his company again.

The night was soft and warm, but in between the explosions and the roar of the onlookers the conversation between them was as easy as it had always been, even if initially Suleiman had seemed startled by the dramatic change that six years had wrought on her appearance.

'How old are you now?' he'd questioned, after he'd looked her up and down for a distractingly long moment.

'I'm eighteen.' She had smiled straight into his eyes, successfully hiding the hurt that he hadn't even remembered her age. 'And all grown up.'

'All grown up,' he had repeated slowly, as if she'd just said something which had never occurred to him before.

The conversation had moved on to other topics, though she had still been conscious of the curious expression in his eyes. He had asked her about her life at boarding school and she'd told him that she was planning to go to art school.

'In England?'

'Of course in England. There is no equivalent here in Dhi'ban.'

'But Dhi'ban isn't the same without you here, Sara.'

It was a strangely emotional thing for Suleiman to say and maybe the unexpectedness of that was what made her reach up to touch her fingertips to his cheek. 'Is that in a good way, or a bad way?' she teased.

A look passed between them and she felt him stiffen.

The fireworks seemed to stop—or maybe that was because the crashing of her heart was as deafening as any man-made explosion in the sky.

He caught hold of her hand and moved it away from his face, and suddenly Sara could feel a terrible yearning as he looked down at her. The normally authoritative Suleiman seemed frozen with indecision and he shook his head, as if he was trying to deny something. And then, almost in slow motion—he lowered his head to brush his lips over hers in a kiss.

It was just like all the books said it should be.

Her world splintered into something magical as their lips met. Suddenly there were rainbows and starlight and a deep, wild hunger. And the realisation that this was her darling, darling Suleiman and he was *kissing* her. Her lips opened beneath his and he circled her waist with his hands as he pulled her closer. She clung to him as her breasts pressed against his broad chest. She heard him groan. She felt the growing tension in his body as his hands moved down to cup her buttocks.

'Oh, Suleiman,' she whispered against his mouth—and the words must have broken the spell, for suddenly he tore himself away from her and held her at arm's length.

For a long moment he just stared at her, his breathing hard and laboured—looking as if he had just been shaken by something profound. Something which made a wild little flicker of hope flare in her heart. But then the look disappeared and was replaced with an expression of self-contempt. It seemed to take a moment or two before he could speak.

'Is this how you behave when you are in England?' he demanded, his voice as deadly as snake poison. 'Offering yourself as freely as a whore when you are promised to the Sultan? What kind of woman are you, Sara?'

It was a question she couldn't answer because she didn't know. Right then, she didn't seem to know anything because her whole belief system seemed to have been shattered. She hadn't been expecting to kiss him, nor to respond to him like that. She hadn't been expecting to want him to touch her in a way she'd never been touched before—yet now he was looking at her as if she'd done something unspeakable.

Filled with shame, she had turned on her heel and fled—her eyes so blurred with tears that she could barely see. And it wasn't until the next day that she heard indulgent tales of the princess weeping with joy for her newly crowned brother.

The memory cleared and Sara found herself in the uncomfortable present, looking into Suleiman's mocking eyes and realising that he was waiting for some sort of answer to his question. Struggling to remember what he'd asked, she shrugged—as if she could shrug off those feelings of humiliation and rejection she had suffered at his hands.

'I hardly describe being a "creative" in an advertising agency as being an executive,' she said.

'You are *creative* in many fields,' he observed. 'Particularly with your choice of clothes. Such revealing, western clothes, I cannot help but notice.'

Sara felt herself stiffen as he began to study her. *Don't look at me that way,* she wanted to scream. Because it was making her body ache as his gaze swept over the sweater dress which came halfway down her thighs, and the high boots whose soft leather curved over her knees.

'I'm glad you like them,' she said flippantly.

'I didn't say I liked them,' he growled. 'In fact, I wholeheartedly disapprove of them, as no doubt would the Sultan. Your dress is ridiculously short, though I suppose that is deliberate.'

'But everyone wears short skirts round here, Suleiman. It's the fashion. And the thick tights and boots almost cancel out the length of the dress, don't you think?'

His eyes were implacable as they met hers. 'I have not come here to discuss the length of your clothes and the way you seem to flaunt your body like the whore we both know you are!'

'No? Then why are you here?'

There was a pause and now his eyes were deadly as they iced into her.

'I think you know the answer to that. But since you seem to have trouble facing up to your responsibilities, maybe I'd better spell it out for you so that there can be no more confusion. You can no longer ignore your destiny, for the time has come.'

'It's not my destiny!' she flared.

'I have come to take you to Qurhah to be married,' he said coldly. 'To fulfil the promise which was made many moons ago by your father. You were sold to the Sultan and the Sultan wants you. And what is more, he is beginning to grow impatient—for this long-awaited alliance between your two countries to go ahead and bring lasting peace in the region.'

Sara froze. The hands which were still concealed in her lap now clenched into two tight fists. She felt beads of sweat break out on her brow and for a moment she thought she might pass out. Because hadn't she thought that if she just ignored the dark cloud which hung over her future for long enough, one day it might just fade away?

'You can't mean that,' she said, hating her voice for sounding so croaky. *So get some strength back. Find the resources within you to stand up to this ridiculous regime which buys women as if they were simply objects of desire lined up on a market stall.* She drew in a deep breath. 'But even if you do mean it, I'm not coming back with you, Suleiman. No way. I live in England now and I regard myself as an English citizen, with all the corresponding freedom that brings. And nothing in the world you can do or say will induce me to go to Qurhah. I don't want to marry the Sultan, and I won't do it. And what is more, you can't make me.'

'I am hoping to do this without a fight, Sara.'

His voice was smooth. As smooth as treacle—and just as dark. But nobody could have mistaken the steely intent which ran through his words. She looked into the flatness of his eyes. She looked at the hard, compromising lines of his lips and she felt another whisper of foreboding shivering its way down her spine. 'You think I'm just going to docilely agree to your plans? That I'm going to nod my head and accompany you to Qurhah?'

'I'm hoping you will, since that would be the most sensible outcome for all concerned.'

'In your dreams, Suleiman.'

There was silence for a moment as Suleiman met the belligerent glitter of her eyes, and the slow rage which had been simmering all day now threatened to boil over. Had he thought that this would be easy?

No, of course he hadn't.

Inside he had known that this would be the most difficult assignment of his life—even though he had experienced battle and torture and real hardship. He had tried to turn the job down—for all kinds of reasons. He'd told the Sultan that he was busy with his new life—and that much was true. But loyalty and affection for his erstwhile employer had proved too persuasive. And who else possessed the right amount of determination to bring the feisty Sara Williams back to marry the royal ruler? His mouth hardened and he felt the twist of something like regret. Who else knew her the way that he did?

'You speak with such insolence that I can only assume you have been influenced by the louche values of the West,' he snapped.

'Embracing freedom, you mean?'

'Embracing disrespect would be a more accurate description.' He drew in a deep breath and forced his lips into something resembling a smile. 'Look, Sara—I understand that you needed to…what is it that you women say? Ah yes, to *find yourself*.' He gave a low laugh. 'Fortunately, the male of the species rarely loses himself in the first place and so such recovery is seldom deemed necessary.'

'Why, you arrogant piece of—'

'Now we can do this one of two ways.' His words cut through her insult like a honed Qurhahian knife. 'The easy way, or the hard way.'

'You mean we do it your way, rather than mine?'

'Bravo—that is exactly what I mean. If you behave reasonably—like a woman who wishes to bring no shame onto her own royal house, or the one you will embrace after your marriage to the Sultan—then everyone is happy.'

'*Happy?*' she echoed. 'Are you out of your mind?'

'There is no need for hysteria,' he said repressively. 'Our journey to Qurhah may not be an expedition which either of us would choose, but I don't see why we can't conduct ourselves in a relatively civilised manner if we put our minds to it.'

'Civilised?' Sara stood up and pushed herself away from the desk so violently that a whole pile of coloured felt-tips fell clattering to the ground. But she barely registered the noise or the mess. She certainly didn't bend down to pick them up and not just because her skirt was so short. She felt a flare of rage and *impotence*—that Suleiman could just march in here as if he owned the place. Start flexing his muscles and telling her—*telling* her—that she must go back and marry a man she barely knew, didn't particularly like and certainly didn't *love*.

'You think it's civilised to hold a woman to a promise of marriage made when she was little more than a child? A forced marriage in which she had no say?'

'Your father himself agreed to this marriage,' said Suleiman implacably. 'You know that.'

'My father had no choice!' she flared. 'He was almost bankrupt by that point!'

'I'm afraid that your father's weakness and profligacy put him in that position. And let us not forget that it was the Sultan's father who saved him from certain bankruptcy!'

'By demanding my hand for his only son, in return?' she demanded. 'What kind of a man could do that, Suleiman?'

She saw that her heartfelt appeal had momentarily stilled him. That his flat black eyes had narrowed and were now partially obscured by the thick ebony lashes which had shuttered down to veil them. Had she been able to make him see the sheer lunacy of his proposal in this day and age? Couldn't he see that it was barbaric for a woman of twenty-three to be taken back to a desert kingdom—no matter how fabled—and to be married against her will?

Once Suleiman had regarded her fondly—she knew that. If he allowed himself to forget that stupid kiss—that single lapse which should never have happened—then surely there still existed in his heart some of that same fondness. Surely he wasn't happy for her to enter into such a barbaric union.

'These dynastic marriages have always taken place,' he said slowly. 'It will not be as bad as you envisage, Sara—'

'Really? How do you work that out?'

'It is a great honour to marry such a man as the Sultan,' he said, but he seemed to be having to force some kind of conviction into his words. He gave a heavy sigh. 'Do you have any idea of the number of women who would long to become his Sultana—'

'A sultana is something I put on my muesli every morning!' she spat back.

'You will be prized above all women,' he continued. 'And given the honour of bearing His Imperial Majesty's sons and heirs. What woman could ask for more?'

For a moment Sara didn't speak, she was so angry. The idea of such a marriage sounded completely abhorrent to her now, but, as Suleiman had just said, she had grown up in a world where such a barter was considered normal. She had been living in England for so long that it was easy to forget that she was herself a royal princess. That her English mother had married a desert king and produced a son and a much younger daughter.

If her mother had been alive she would have stopped this ludicrous marriage from happening, Sara was sure of that. But her mother had been dead for a long time— her father, too. And now the Sultan wanted to claim what was rightfully his.

She thought of the man who awaited her and she shivered. She knew that a lot of women thought of him as a swarthy sex-god, but she wasn't among them. During their three, heavily chaperoned meetings—she had felt nothing for him. Nada.

But mightn't that have had something to do with the fact that Suleiman had been present all those times? Suleiman with his glittering black eyes and his hard, honed body who had distracted her so badly that she couldn't think straight.

She glared at him. 'Doesn't it strike at your conscience to take a woman back to Qurhah *against her will*? Do you always do whatever the Sultan asks you, without questioning it? His tame puppet!'

A nerve flickered at his temple. 'I no longer work for the Sultan.'

For a moment she stared at him in disbelief. 'What... what are you talking about? The Sultan values you above all other men. Everyone knows that. You are his prized emissary and the man on whom he relies.'

He shook his head. 'Not any longer. I have returned to my own land, where I have built a different kind of life for myself.'

She wanted to ask him what kind of life that was, but

she reminded herself that what Suleiman did was none of her business. *He doesn't want you. He doesn't even seem to like you any more.* 'Then why are you here?'

'As a favour to Murat. He thought that you might prove too much of a challenge for most of his staff.'

'But not for you, I suppose?'

'Not for me,' he agreed.

She wanted to tell him to wipe that smug smile off his face and get out of her office and if he didn't, then she would call security and get them to remove him. But was that such a good idea? Her eyes flickered doubtfully over his powerful body and immovable stance. Was she seriously suggesting that *anyone* could budge him if he didn't want to go?

She thought about her boss. Wouldn't Gabe Steel have Suleiman evicted from the building if she asked him? Though when she stopped to think about it—did she really want to go bleating to her boss for help? She had no desire to blight her perfect working record by bringing her private life into the workplace. Because wouldn't Gabe—and all her colleagues—be amazed to discover that she wasn't just someone called Sara Williams, but a half-blood desert princess from the desert country of Dhi'ban? That she had capitalised on her mother's English looks and used her mother's English surname to blend in since she'd been working here in London. And blend in, she had—adopting the fashions and the attitudes of other English women her age.

No, this was not a time for opposition—or at least, not a time for *open* opposition. She didn't want Suleiman's suspicions alerted. She needed to lull him.

To let him think that he had won. That she would go with him—not *too* meekly or he would suspect that something was amiss, but that she *would* go with him.

She shrugged her shoulders as if she were reluctantly conceding victory and backed it up with a resigned sigh. 'I suppose there's no point in me trying to change your mind?'

His smile was cold. 'Do you really think you could?'

'No, I suppose not,' she said, as if his indifference didn't matter. As if she didn't care what he thought of her.

But she felt as if somebody had just taken her dreams and trampled on them. He was the only man she had ever wanted. The only man she'd ever loved. Yet Suleiman thought so little of her that he could just hand her over to another man, as if she were a parcel he was delivering.

'Don't look like that, Sara.' His black eyes narrowed and she saw that little muscle flicker at his temple once more. 'If you open your mind a little—you might find that you can actually enjoy your new life. That you can be a good wife. You will have strong sons and beautiful daughters and this will make the people of Qurhah very happy.'

For a moment, Sara thought she heard the hint of uncertainty in his voice. As if he was trotting out the official line without really believing it. Was he? Or was it true what they said—that something in his own upbringing had hardened his heart so that it was made of stone? So that he didn't care about other people's feelings—because he didn't have any of his own.

Well, Suleiman's feelings were none of her business. She didn't care about them because she couldn't afford to. She needed to know what his plans were—and how to react to them accordingly.

'So what happens now?' she asked casually. 'Do I give a month's notice here and then fly out to Qurhah towards the end of January?'

His mouth twisted, as if she had just said something uniquely funny. 'You think that you are free to continue to make the Sultan wait for your presence?' he questioned. 'I'm afraid that those days are over. You will fly out to Qurhah tonight. And you are leaving this building with me, right now.'

Panic—pure and simple—overwhelmed her. She could feel the doors of the prison clanging to a close. Suleiman's dark features blurred for a second, before clicking back into sharp focus, and she tried to pull herself together.

'I'll...I'll need to pack first,' she said.

'Of course.' He inclined his dark head but not before she could see the sudden glint of fire in his eyes. 'Though I doubt whether your mini-skirt will cut it in your new role as Sultana. A far more suitable wardrobe will be provided for you, so why bother?'

'I'm not talking about my clothes!' she flared back. 'Surely you won't deny me my trinkets and keepsakes? The jewellery my mother left me and the book my father published after her death?'

For a moment she wondered if she had imagined the faint look of disquiet which briefly flickered in his eyes. But it was gone as quickly as it had appeared and she told herself to stop attributing thoughts and feelings to him, just because she wanted him to have them. Because he didn't.

'Very well,' he said. 'That can be arranged. Now let's go—I have a car waiting downstairs.'

Sara's heart missed a beat. Of course he had a car waiting. Probably with a couple of heavies inside. That feeling of being trapped closed in on her again and suddenly she knew that she wasn't going to take this lying down. She would not go meekly with Suleiman Abd al-Aziz—she would slip through his hands like an eel plucked from an icy river.

'I have to finish up in here,' she said. 'I can't just walk out for ever without putting my work in some kind of order.'

His face was unreadable. 'How long will it take?'

Sara felt her mouth dry as she wondered realistically how much time she could plead to play with. 'A few hours?'

'Don't test my patience, Sara. Two hours will be more than adequate for what you need to do. I will be waiting with my men at your apartment.' He walked over to the door and paused. 'And don't be late,' he said softly.

With one final warning flickering from his black eyes, he was gone. She waited until she heard the ping of the lift in the corridor and the sound of the elevator doors closing—but she was still paranoid enough to poke her head outside the office to check that he really *had* gone. That he wasn't standing in the shadows spying on her and waiting to see what she would do next.

She shut the office door and walked over to one of
the giant windows which overlooked the dark glitter
of the river, feeling a stab of pain in her heart. She had
loved working here. She had loved the freedom and
the creativity of being part of Gabe Steel's enormous
organisation.

But now it was all coming to an end, whether she
wanted it to or not.

Like hell it was.

An idea began to form in her mind. A plan so auda-
cious that for a moment she wondered if she dared go
ahead with it. Yet what choice did she have? To go with
Suleiman, like a sheep to the slaughter? To be forced
to share a bed with the hawk-faced Sultan—a man for
whom she had felt not one whisper of chemistry?

She picked up the office phone instead of her own
mobile phone. Because if they'd had bodyguards
watching her all this time—who was to say they hadn't
bugged her phone?

It didn't take her long to get the information she
wanted from the Business Development Director, who
was in charge of the company's public relations. Judging by the noise in the background, he was clearly at
some sort of Christmas party and gave her a list of
journalists without asking any questions.

Her fingers were trembling as she dialled the first
number and listened to the ring tone. Maybe nobody
would pick up. Maybe they'd all set off home for
Christmas—all going to some storybook destination
with a wreath on the door and a roaring log fire, with
the smell of chestnuts and pine scenting the air.

They wouldn't be spending their Christmas Eve like her—with a car full of cold-faced men sitting outside the building, waiting to take her away to an unknown and unwanted future.

'Hello?'

She took a deep breath. 'Look, I know this is going to sound crazy—but I've got a story you might be interested in.' Her fingers dug into the phone as she listened. 'Details? Sure I can give you details. How about the proposed kidnap of a woman, who is being taken against her will to the desert country of Qurhah to marry a man she doesn't want to marry? You like that? I rather thought you might—and it's all yours. An exclusive. But we haven't got long. I need to leave London before six o' clock.'

CHAPTER TWO

SULEIMAN BROUGHT THE car to a halt so that it was hidden beneath the shadows of the trees, but still within sight of the cottage. The other cars all waited in darkness at various intervals down the country lane, as he had instructed them to do.

He turned off the lights. Rain spattered relentlessly across the windscreen, running in thick rivulets down the glass. For a moment he sat watching the lighted windows of the house. He saw Sara's unmistakable silhouette going around, pulling the drapes tightly shut, and he felt a potent combination of anger and satisfaction. But alongside his triumph at having tracked her down, a deep disquiet ran through his veins like slow poison.

He should have refused this job.

He should have told Murat that his schedule did not allow him time to travel to England and deal with the princess.

But the Sultan did not ask favours of many men and the bonds of loyalty and gratitude ran deeper than Suleiman had anticipated. And although he would have given anything to have avoided this particular task, somehow he had found himself accepting it. Yet just one sight of her today had reinforced what a fool he had been. Better to have thrown himself to the mercy of a starving lion, than to have willingly closeted himself with the temptress Sara.

He remembered the honeyed taste of her lips and her intoxicating perfume of jasmine mixed with patchouli. He remembered the pert thrust of her breast beneath his questing fingers and the way his body had ached for her afterwards. The frustrated lust which seemed to have gone on for months.

His hands tightened around the steering wheel. Women like her were born to create trouble. To make men want them and then to use their sexual power to destroy them. Hadn't her own mother—a fabled beauty in her time—brought down the king who had spent his life in slavish devotion to her? A husband who had spent so much time enthralled by her that he had barely noticed his country slipping into bankruptcy.

He drew in a deep, meditative breath, forcing all the frustrating thoughts from his mind. He must go and do what he needed to do and then leave and never see her again.

With a stealth nurtured by years of undercover work, he waited until he was certain the coast was clear before he got out of the car and silently pulled the door shut behind him. He saw one of the limousines parked further down the lane flash its lights at him.

Avoiding the crunch of the gravel path, he felt his shoes sink into the sodden mud of the lawn which ran alongside it. But the night was fearsome and the weather atrocious and he was soaked within seconds, despite his long-legged stride towards the front door.

He was half tempted to break in by one of the back windows and then to walk in and confront her to show just how vulnerable she really was. But that would be cruel and he had no desire to be cruel to her.

Did he?

His mouth hardened as he lifted one rain-soaked hand to the door handle and knocked.

If she was sensible, she wouldn't answer. Instead, she would phone the local police station and tell them she had an intruder banging on the door of this isolated cottage on Christmas Eve.

But clearly she wasn't being sensible because he could hear the sound of her approaching footsteps and his body tensed as adrenalin flooded through him.

She pulled open the door, her violet eyes widening as she registered his identity. For a split second she reacted quickly, trying desperately to shut the door again—but her reactions were not as fast as his. Few people's were. He placed the flat of his hand on the weathered knocker and blocked her move until she had the sense to step back as he entered the hallway, pushing the door shut behind him.

For a moment there was silence in that small hall-way, other than the soft drip of rainwater onto the stone tiles. He could see that she was too stunned to speak—and so was he, but for very different reasons. She might be regarding him with horror but no such feelings were dominating his own mind right then.

She had changed from the provocative dress she'd been wearing in her office earlier. Her hair was loose and her jeans and pink sweater were not particularly clingy, yet still they managed to showcase the magnificence of her body.

He knew it was wrong but he couldn't stop himself from drinking her in, like a man lost in the desert who had just been handed a jug of cool water. Was she aware of her beauty? Of the fact that she looked like a goddess? A goddess in blue jeans.

'Suleiman!' Her voice sounded startled and her violet eyes were dark.

'Surprised?' he questioned.

'You could say that! And horrified.' She glared at him. 'What do you think you're doing—pushing your way in here like some sort of heavy?'

'I thought we had an appointment to meet at six, but since it is now almost eight, you appear to have broken it. Shockingly bad manners, Sara. Especially for a future queen of the desert.'

'Tough!' she retorted. 'And I'm not going to be a queen of the desert. I already told you that I have no intention of getting married. Not to Murat and not to anyone! So why waste everybody's time by turning up? Can't you just go back to the Sultan and tell him to forget the whole idea?'

Suleiman heard the determination in her voice and felt an unwilling flare of admiration for her unashamed—and very stupid—defiance. Such open insubordination was unheard of from a woman from the desert lands and it was rather magnificent to observe her spirited rebellion. But he didn't let it show. Instead, he injected a note of disapproval into his voice. 'I am waiting for an explanation about why you failed to show.'

'Do you realise you sound exactly like a schoolteacher? I don't really think you'd need to be a detective to work out my no-show. I don't like having my arm twisted.'

'Clearly you hadn't thought things through properly, if you imagined it was going to be that easy to shake me off,' he said. 'But you're here now.'

She eyed him speculatively 'I could knock you over the back of the head and make a run for it.'

His mouth quirked at the corners, despite all his best efforts not to smile. 'And if you did, you would run straight into the men I have positioned all the way down the lane. Don't even think about it, Sara. And please don't imagine that I haven't thought of every eventuality, because I have.'

He pulled off his dripping coat and hung it on a peg.

She glared at him. 'I don't remember asking you to take your coat off!'

'I don't require your permission.'

'You are impossible!' she hissed.

'I have never denied that.'

'*Oh,*' she said, her voice frustrated as she turned round and marched towards a room where he could see a fire blazing.

He followed her into a room which had none of the ornaments the English were so fond of cramming into their country homes. There were no china dogs or hangings made of brass. No jumbled oil paintings of ships which hinted at a naval past. Instead, the walls were pale and contrasted with the weathered beams of wood in the ceiling. The furniture was quirky but looked comfortable and the few contemporary paintings worked well, though in theory they shouldn't have done. Whoever owned this had taste, as well as money.

'Whose cottage is this?' he questioned.

'My lover's.'

He took a step forward, so that his shadow fell over her defiant features. 'Please don't jest with me, Sara. I'm not in the mood for it.'

'How do you know I'm jesting?'

'I hope you are. Because if I thought for a moment that you had been intimate with another man—then I would seek him out and tear him from limb to limb.'

As she heard his venomous but undoubtedly truthful words Sara swallowed, reminding herself that it wasn't a question of Suleiman being jealous. He had only uttered the threat out of loyalty to the Sultan.

She wished he hadn't turned up and yet if she'd stopped to think about it for more than a second—she must have known he would follow her. If Suleiman took on a task, then Suleiman would see it through. No matter what obstacles were put before him, he would conquer them. *That* was why the Sultan had asked him—and why he was so respected and feared within the desert nations.

She had driven here without really thinking about the consequences of her action, only about her urgent need to get away. Not just from the dark certainty of her future, but from this man. The man who had rejected her, yet could still make her heart race with desire and longing.

But his face was as cold as a stone mask. His body language was tense and forbidding. Suleiman's feelings towards her had clearly not changed since the night he'd kissed her and then thrust her away from him. She swallowed. How could she bear to spend hours travelling with him, towards a dark fate which seemed unendurable?

'It's my boss, Gabe Steel's cottage,' she said. 'And how did you find me?'

'It wasn't difficult,' he said. 'You forget that I have tracked down quarry far more elusive than a stubborn princess. Actually, it was your sudden unexpected consent to my plan which alerted my suspicions. It is not like you to be so *acquiescent,* Sara. I suspected that you would try to give my men the slip so I hid outside the side entrance to your office block and followed you to the car park.'

'You *hid*? Outside my office block?'

'You find that so bizarre?'

'Of course I do!' Her heart was hammering in her chest. 'I live in England now and I live an English life, Suleiman. One where men don't usually lurk in shadows, following women who don't want to be followed. Why, you could have been arrested for trespass—especially if my boss had any idea that you were *stalking* me.'

'Unlikely—for I am never seen if I do not wish to be seen,' he said arrogantly. 'You must have known it was a futile attempt to try to escape, so why do it, Sara? Did you really think you could get away with it?'

'Go to hell!'

'I'm not going anywhere and certainly not without you.'

She hated the ruthless tone of his voice. She hated the unresponsive look on his hard face. Suddenly she wanted to shake him. To provoke him. To get some sort of reaction which would make her feel as if she was dealing with a real person, instead of a cold block of stone. 'I was waiting here,' she said deliberately. 'For my lover.'

'I don't think so.'

'And why not?' she demanded. 'Am I so repulsive that you can't imagine that a man might actually want to take me to bed?'

For a moment Suleiman stilled, telling himself that he wouldn't fall into the trap she was so obviously laying for him. She was trying to rile him. Trying to get him to admit to something he was not prepared to admit. Even to himself. Concentrate on the facts, he told himself fiercely—and not on her blonde-haired beauty, or her soft curves which nature must have invented with the intention of sending any man crazy with longing.

'I think you know the answer to that question—and I'm not going to flatter your ego by answering it. Your desirability has never been in question, but you seem to imply that your virtue is.'

'What if it is?' she challenged, her voice growing reckless. 'But I don't have to explain myself to you and

I'm certainly not going to take orders from you. Do you want to know why?'

'Not really,' he said, in a bored tone.

'I think you might.' She licked her lips in a cat-got-the-cream expression and then smiled. 'It might interest you to know that in between your invasion of my office and following me here, I have spoken to a journalist.'

There was a pause. Suleiman's eyes narrowed. 'I hope that's a joke.'

'It's not.'

There was another moment of silence before he could bring himself to speak. 'And what did you tell the journalist?'

She scraped her fingers back through her blonde hair and smirked. 'I told him the truth. No need to look so scared, Suleiman. I mean, who in their right mind could possibly object to the truth?'

'Let's get one thing straight,' he said, biting the words out from between gritted teeth. 'I am not scared—of anyone or anything. I think you may be in danger of mistaking my anger for fear, though perhaps you would do well to feel fear yourself. Because if the Sultan finds out that you have spoken to the western press, then things are going to get very tricky. So I shall ask you again and this time I want a straight answer—what exactly did you tell the journalist?'

Sara stared into the spitting blackness of his eyes and some of her bravado wavered, until she told herself that she wasn't going to be intimidated. She had worked too hard and too long to forge a new life to allow these powerful men to control her. These desert men who would crush your very spirit if you allowed them to do so. So she wouldn't let them.

Even her own mother—who had married a desert king and had loved him—had felt imprisoned by ancient royal rules which hadn't changed for centuries and probably never would. Sara had witnessed for herself that sometimes love just wasn't enough. So what chance would a marriage have if there was no love at all?

Her mother's unhappiness had been the cause of her father's ruination—and had ultimately governed Sara's own fate. She hadn't known that Papa was so obsessed by his English wife that he hadn't paid proper attention to governing his country. Sara remembered that all too vividly. The Queen had been his possession and nothing else had really existed for him, apart from that.

He had taken his eye off the ball. Poor investments and a border war which went on too long meant that his country was left bankrupt. The late Sultan of Qurhah had come up with a deal for a bail-out plan and the price had been Sara's hand in marriage.

When Sara's mother had died and she had been allowed to go off to boarding school—hadn't she thought that her father's debt would just be allowed to fade with time? Hadn't she been naïve and hopeful enough to think that the Sultan might just forget all about marrying her, as his own father had decreed he should?

Blinking back the sudden threat of tears, Sara tried to ignore the fierce expression on Suleiman's face. She was *not* going to be made to feel guilty—when all she was doing was trying to save her own skin. And ultimately she would be doing the Sultan a favour—for surely it would damage the ego of such a powerful man if she was forced kicking and screaming to the altar.

'I am waiting,' he said, with silky venom, 'for you to enlighten me. What did you tell the journalist, Sara?'

She met the accusation in his eyes. 'I told him everything.'

'Everything?'

'Yes! I thought it would make a good story,' she said. 'At a time of year when newspapers are traditionally very light on news and—'

'What did you tell him?' he raged.

'I told him the truth! That I was a half-blood princess—half English and half Dhi'banese. You know the papers—they just love any kind of royal connection!' She forced a mocking smile, knowing that it would irritate him and wondering if irritating him was only a feeble attempt to suppress her desire for him. Because if it was, it wasn't working. 'I told him that my mother travelled as an artist to Dhi'ban, to paint the beautiful desert landscape—and that my father, the king, had fallen in love with her.'

'Why did you feel it necessary to parade your private family history to a complete stranger?'

'I'm just providing the backstory, Suleiman,' she said. 'Everyone knows you need a good backstory if you want an entertaining read. Anyway, it's all there on record.'

'You are severely testing my patience,' he said. 'You had no right to divulge these things!'

'Surely the Sultan wouldn't mind me discussing it?' she questioned innocently. 'This is a marriage we're talking about, Suleiman—and marriages are supposed to be happy occasions. I say *supposed* to be, but that's quite a difficult concept to pull off when the bride is being kidnapped! I have to say that the journalist seemed quite surprised when I told him that I had no say in this marriage. No, when I come to think of it— surprise is the wrong word. I'd say that astonished covered it better. And deeply shocked, of course.'

'Shocked?'

'Mmm. He seemed to find it odd—abhorrent, even—that the Sultan of Qurhah should want to marry a woman who had been bought for him by his own father!'

She saw his fists clench.

'That is the way of the world you were brought into,' he said unequivocally. 'None of us can change the circumstances of our birth.'

'No, we can't. But that doesn't mean we have to be made prisoners by it. We can use everything in our power to change our destinies! Can't you see that, Suleiman?'

'No!'

'Yes,' she argued passionately. 'Yes and a thousand times yes!' Her heart began to race as she saw something written on his carved features which made her stomach turn to jelly. Was it anger? Was it?

But anger would not have made him shake his head, as if he was trying to shake off thoughts of madness. Nor to make that little nerve flicker so violently at his olive-skinned temple. He took a step towards her and, for one heart-stopping moment, she thought he was about to pull her into his arms, the way he'd done on the night of her brother's coronation.

And didn't she want that? Wasn't she longing for him to do just that, only this time not stop? This time they were alone and he could lie her down in front of that log fire and loosen her clothes and...

But he didn't touch her. He stood a tantalisingly close distance away while his eyes sparked dark fire at her. She could see him swallowing, as if he had something bitter lodged in his throat.

'You must accept your destiny,' he said. 'As I have accepted mine.'

'Have you? Did "accepting your destiny" include kissing me on the night my brother was crowned, even though you knew I was promised to another?'

'Don't say that!'

The strangled words sounded almost *powerless* and Sara realised she'd never heard Suleiman sound like that before. Not even after he'd returned from his undercover duties in the Qurhah army, when he'd been thirty pounds lighter with a scar zigzagging down his neck. People said he'd been tortured, but if he had he never spoke of it—well, never to her. She remembered being profoundly shocked by his appearance and she felt a similar kind of shock washing over her now.

For it was not like looking at Suleiman she knew of old. It was like looking at a stranger. A repressed and forbidding stranger. His features had closed up and his eyes were hooded. Had she really thought he was about to kiss her? Why, kissing looked like the furthest thing on his mind.

'We will not speak of that night again,' he said.

'But it's true, isn't it?' she questioned. 'You weren't so moralistic when you touched me like that.'

'Because most men would have died rather than resist you that night,' he admitted bitterly. 'And I chose not to die. I hadn't seen you for six long years and then I saw you, with your big painted eyes and your silver gown, shining like the moon.'

Briefly, Suleiman closed his eyes, because that kiss had been like no other, no matter how much he had tried to deny it. It hadn't just been about sex or lust. It had been much more powerful than that, and infinitely more dangerous. It had been about feeding a hunger as fundamental as the need to eat or drink. It had felt as necessary as breathing. And yet it had angered him, because it had seemed outside his control. Up until that moment he had regarded the young princess with nothing more than indulgent friendship. What had happened that night had taken him completely by surprise. He swallowed. Perhaps that was why it had been the most unforgettable kiss of his life.

'Didn't you realise how much I wanted you that night, Sara, even though you were promised to the Sultan? Were you not aware of your own power?'

'So it was all my fault?'

'No. It is not your "fault" that you looked beautiful enough to test the appetites of a saint. I blame no one but myself for my unforgivable weakness. But it is a weakness which will never be repeated,' he ground out. 'And yes, I blame you if you have now given an interview which will bring shame on the reputation of the Sultan and his royal house.'

'Then ask him to set me free,' she said simply. 'To let me go. Please, Suleiman.'

Suleiman met the appeal in her big violet eyes and for a moment he almost wavered. For wasn't it a terrible crime to see the beautiful and spirited Sara forced to marry a man she did not love? Could he really imagine her lying in the marital bed and submitting to the embraces of a man she claimed not to want? And then he told himself that Murat was a legendary lover. And even though it made him feel sick to acknowledge it—it was unlikely that Sara would lie unresponsive in Murat's bed for too long.

'I can't do that,' he said, but the words felt like stone as he let them fall from his lips. 'I can't allow you to reject the Sultan; I would be failing in my duty if I did. It is a question of pride.'

'Pride!' Angrily, she shook her head. 'What price pride? What if I refuse to allow him to consummate the marriage?' she challenged. 'What then? Won't he skulk away to his harem and take his pleasure elsewhere?'

He flinched as if she had hit him. 'This discussion has become completely inappropriate,' he bit out angrily. 'But you would be wise to consider the effect of your actions on your brother, the King—even though I know you never bother to visit him. There are some in your country who wonder whether the King still has a sister, so rarely does she set foot in her homeland.'

'My relationship with my brother is none of your business—and neither are my trips home!'

'Maybe not. But you would do well to remember that Qurhah continues to shoulder some of your country's national debt. How would your brother feel if the Sultan were to withdraw his financial support because of your behaviour?'

'You *bastard*,' she hissed, but she might as well have been whispering on the wind, for all the notice he took.

'My skin is thick enough to withstand your barbed comments, princess. I am delivering you to the Sultan and nothing will prevent that. But first, I want the name of the journalist you've been dealing with.'

She made one last stab at rebellion. 'And if I won't tell you?'

'Then I will find out for myself,' he said, in a tone which made a shiver trickle down her spine. 'Why not save me the time and yourself my anger?'

'You're a brute,' she breathed. 'An egocentric brute.'

'No, Sara, I just want the story spiked.'

Frustration washed over her as she recognised that he meant business. And that she was fighting a useless battle here.

'His name is Jason Cresswell,' she said sulkily. 'He works for the *Daily View.*'

'Good. Perhaps you are finally beginning to see sense. You might learn that co-operation is infinitely more preferable to rebellion. Now leave me while I speak with him in private.' He glanced at her as he pulled his mobile phone from his pocket.

'Go and get your coat on. Because after I've finished with the journalist we're heading for the airfield, where the plane is waiting to take you to your new life in Qurhah.'

CHAPTER THREE

THE FLIGHT WAS smooth and the aircraft supremely comfortable but Suleiman couldn't sleep. For the past seven hours during the journey to Qurhah, he had been kept awake by the tormenting thoughts of what he was doing.

He felt his heart clench. What *was* he doing?

Taking a woman to a man she did not love.

A woman he wanted for himself.

Restlessly, he moved noiselessly around the craft, wishing that there were somewhere to look other than at the sleeping Sara. But although he could have joined the two pilots in the cockpit or tried to rest in the sealed-off section at the far end of the plane, neither option appealed. He couldn't seem to tear his eyes away from her.

He wondered if the silent female servants who were sitting sentry had noticed the irresistible direction of his gaze. Or the fact that he had not left the side of the sleeping princess. But he didn't care—for who would dare challenge him?

He had fulfilled the first part of his task by getting

Sara on board the plane. He just wished he could shake off this damned feeling of *guilt*.

Their late exit from the cottage into the driving rain had left her soaking wet for she had stubbornly refused to use the umbrella he'd opened for her. And as she had sat shivering beside him in the car he'd fought the powerful urge to pull her into his arms and to rub at her cold flesh until she was warm again. But he had vowed that he would not touch her again.

He could never touch her again.

He let his eyes drift over her.

Stretched out in the wide aircraft seat in her crumpled jeans and sweater, she should have looked unremarkable but that was the very last thing she looked. He felt his gut tighten. The sculpted angles of her bone structure hinted at her aristocratic lineage and her eyelashes were naturally dark. Even her blonde hair, which had dried into tousled strands, looked like layered starlight.

She was beautiful.

The most beautiful woman he'd ever seen.

His heart clenched as he turned away, but his troubled thoughts continued to plague him.

He knew the Sultan's reputation. He knew that he was a charismatic man where women were concerned and that most of his former lovers still yearned for him. But Murat the Mighty was a desert man and he believed in destiny. He would marry the princess who had been chosen for him, for to do otherwise would be to renege on an ancient pact. He would marry and take his new bride back to the Qurhahian palace. He would think nothing of it.

Suleiman winced as he tried to imagine Sara being closed off for ever in the Sultan's gilded world and felt a terrible darkness enter his heart.

He heard the small sound she made as she stirred, blinking open her eyes to look at him so that he found himself staring into dark pools of violet ink.

Sitting up, she pushed her tousled hair away from her face. Was she aware that he had been watching her while she slept, and that it had felt unbelievably intimate to do so? Would she be shocked to know that he had imagined moving aside the cashmere blanket and climbing in beside her?

She lifted her arms above her head to yawn and in that moment she looked so *free* that another wave of guilt washed over him.

What would she be like when she'd had her wings clipped by the pressures and the demands of her new position as Sultana? Did she realise that never again would she wear her faded blue jeans or move around anonymously as she had done in London? Did she realize—as he now did—that this trip was the last time he would ever be permitted to be alone with her?

'You're awake,' he said.

'Top marks for observation,' she said, raking her fingers back through her hair to subdue it. 'Gosh, the Sultan must miss having you around if you come out with inspirational gems like that, Suleiman.'

'Are you going to be impertinent for the rest of the journey?'

'I might. If I feel like it.'

'Would a little tea lighten your mood, princess?'

Sara shrugged, wondering whether anything could lighten her mood at that precise moment. Because this was fast becoming like her worst nightmare. She had been bundled onto the plane, with the Sultan's staff bowing and curtseying to her as soon as she had set foot on the private jet. These days she wasn't used to being treated like a princess and it made her feel uncomfortable. She had seen the surreptitious glances which had come shooting her way. Were they thinking: *Here's the princess who ran away?* Or were they thinking what an unworthy wife she would make for their beloved Sultan?

But the most troubling aspect was not that she was being taken somewhere against her will, to marry a man she didn't love. It was the stupid yearning feeling she got whenever she looked at Suleiman's shuttered features and found herself wishing that he would lose the uptight look and just kiss her. She found herself longing for the closeness of yesteryear, instead of this strange new tenseness which surrounded him.

She could guess *why* he was behaving so coolly towards her, but that didn't seem to alleviate this terrible *aching* which was gnawing away at her heart, despite all her anger and confusion.

'So. How did your "chat" with the journalist go?' she asked. 'Did he agree to kill the story?'

'He did.' He slanted her a triumphant look. 'I managed to convince him that your words were simply a heightened version of the normal nerves of a bride-to-be.'

'So you bribed him, I suppose? Offered him riches beyond his wildest dreams not to publish?'

Suleiman smiled. 'I'm afraid so.'

Frustratedly, Sara sank back against the cushions and watched Suleiman raise his hand in command, instantly bringing one of the servants scurrying over to take his order for tea. He was so *easy* with power, she thought. He acted as if he'd been born to it—which as far as she knew, he hadn't. She knew that he'd been schooled alongside the Sultan, but that was all she *did* know—because he was notoriously cagy about his past. He'd once told her that the strongest men were those who kept their past locked away from prying eyes—and while she could see the logic in that, it had always maddened her that she hadn't known more about what made him tick.

She took a sip of the fragrant camomile brew she was handed before putting her cup down to study him. 'You say you're no longer working for the Sultan?'

'That's right.'

'So what are you doing instead? Doesn't your new boss mind you flitting off to England like this?'

'I don't have a boss. I don't answer to anyone, Sara. I work for myself.'

'Doing what—providing bespoke kidnap services for reluctant brides?'

'I thought we'd agreed to lose the hysteria.'

'Doing what?' she persisted.

Suleiman cracked the knuckles of his fists and

stared down at the whitened bones because that was a far less distracting sight than confronting the spark of interest in those beautiful violet eyes. 'I own an oil refinery and several very lucrative wells.'

'You own an oil refinery?' she repeated in disbelief. 'A baby one?'

'Quite a big one, actually.'

'How on earth can you afford to do that?'

He lifted his head and met the confusion in her gaze. He thought how inevitably skewed her idea of the world was—a world where kingdoms were lost and bought and bartered. His investigations into her London life had assured him that her job for Gabe Steel was bona fide, but he knew that she'd inherited her luxury apartment from her mother. Sara was a princess, he reminded himself grimly. She'd never wanted for anything.

'I played the stock market,' he said.

'Oh, come on—Suleiman. It can't be as simple as that. Loads of people play the stock market, but they don't all end up with oil refineries.'

He leaned back against the silken pile of cushions, an ill-thought-out move, since it put his eye-line on a level with her breasts. Instead, he fixed his gaze on her violet eyes.

'Even as a boy, I was always good with numbers,' he said. 'And later on, I found it almost *creative* to watch the movement of the markets and predict what was going to happen next. It was, if you like, a hobby—a consuming as well as a very profitable one. Over the years I managed to accrue a considerable amount of wealth, which I invested. I bought shares along the way which flourished. Some property here and there.'

'Where?'

'Some in Samahan and some in the Caribbean. But I was looking for something more challenging. On the hunch of a geologist I met on a plane to San Francisco, I began drilling in an area of my homeland which, up until that moment, everyone had thought was barren land. It provided one of the richest oil wells in Middle Eastern history.' He shrugged. 'I was lucky.'

Sara blinked at him, as if there was a fundamental part of the story missing. 'So you had all this money in the bank, yet you continued to work for the Sultan?'

'Why not? There is nothing to match the buzz of being in politics and I'd always enjoyed my role as his envoy.'

'So you did,' she agreed slowly. 'Until one day, something made you leave and start up on your own.'

'If you hadn't been a princess, you could have been a detective,' he said sardonically.

'So what was it, Suleiman? Why the big lifestyle change?'

'Isn't it right and natural that a man should have ambition?' he questioned, taking a sip of his own tea. 'That he should wish to be his own master?'

'What was it, Suleiman?' she repeated quietly.

Suleiman felt his body tense. Should he tell her? Would the truth weaken him in her eyes, or would it make her realise why this damned attraction which still sizzled between them could never be acted upon?

'It was you,' he said. 'You were the catalyst.'

'Me?'

'Yes, you. And why the innocent look of surprise? Haven't you yet learned that every action has a consequence, Sara? Think about it. The night you offered yourself to me—'

'It was a kiss, for heavens sake!' she croaked.

'It was more than a kiss and we both know it,' he continued remorselessly. 'Or are you saying that, if I had pushed you against the shadowed palace wall for yet more intimacy, you would have stopped me?'

'Suleiman!'

'Are you saying that?' he repeated, but he found her blush deeply satisfying—for it spoke of an innocence he had begun to question. And wouldn't it be better to air all his bitterness and frustration so that he could let it out and move on, as he needed to move on? As they both did.

'No,' she said, the word a flat, small admission. 'How can I deny it?'

'I felt shame,' he continued. 'Not so much for what I had done, but for what I wanted to do. I had betrayed the Sultan in the worst way imaginable and I could no longer count myself as his most loyal aide.'

She was looking at him in disbelief. 'So one kiss made you resign?'

He nearly told her the rest, but he stopped himself in time. If he admitted that he couldn't bear to think of her in another man's arms and that he found it intolerable to contemplate her being married to the Sultan and being forced to look on from the sidelines. If he explained that the thought of another man thrusting deep inside her body made him feel sick—then wouldn't that reveal more than it was safe to reveal? Wouldn't it make temptation creep out from behind the shadows?

'It would have been impossible for me to work alongside your new husband with you as his wife,' he said.

'I see.'

And she did see. Or rather, she saw some of it. Sara stared at the black-haired man sitting before her, because now the pieces of the puzzle were beginning to form a more coherent shape. Suleiman had *wanted* her. Really wanted her. And now she was beginning to suspect that he still did. Behind the rigid pose he presented and the wall of disapproval, there still burned *something*. He had all but admitted it just now.

Didn't that explain the way his body tensed whenever she grew close? Why his dark eyes had grown stormy and opaque when he'd studied her short skirt that day in the office. It was not indifference towards her as she had first thought.

It was Suleiman trying to hide the fact that he still wanted her.

She licked her dry lips and saw his eyes follow the movement of her tongue, as if he was being compelled to do something against his will. Was he remembering—as she was—when his own tongue had entered her mouth and made her moan with pleasure?

Her head was spinning; her thoughts were confused but as they began to clear she saw a possible solution to her dilemma. What if she used Suleiman's desire for her to her own advantage? What if she tempted him beyond endurance and *seduced* him, what then? If they finished off what they had started all those years ago, wasn't that a way out for her? He was a single-minded man, yes, and a determined one, but there was no way he could present her to Murat if he had been intimate with her himself.

Could she do it? Could she? She was certainly no seductress, but how difficult could it be to beguile the only man she had ever really wanted?

She rose to her feet. 'Where's the bathroom?' she asked.

'Through there,' he said—pointing towards the door at the far end of the cabin.

She reached up towards the rack to retrieve the bag she'd brought with her and Suleiman moved forward to help, but she shook her head with a sudden fierce show of independence. She might want him, but she didn't need him. She didn't need any man. Wasn't that the whole point of her carefree life in London? That she didn't have to be tied down and trapped. 'I'm perfectly capable of doing it myself.'

She disappeared into the bathroom, emerging a short while later with her blonde hair brushed and woven into a neat chignon. She had changed from her jeans and sweater and replaced them with clothes more suited to the desert climate of Qurhah.

Her slim-fitting linen trousers and long-sleeved silk shirt now covered most of her flesh, but, despite the concealing outfit, she felt curiously *exposed* as she walked back towards him. Her legs were unsteady and her stomach was tying itself up in knots as she sat down. For a moment she couldn't quite bring herself to meet Suleiman's eyes, terrified that he might discover the subversive nature of her thoughts.

'So what happens when we arrive?' she questioned. 'Will an armed guard be taking over from you? Will I be handcuffed, perhaps?'

'We are landing at one of the military airbases,' he said. 'That way, your arrival won't be marred by the curiosity of onlookers at Qurhah's international airport.'

'In case I make a break for freedom, you mean?'

'I thought we'd discounted this rather hysterical approach of yours?' he said. 'And since the threat of desert storms has been brewing for days, it is considered unsafe for us to use a helicopter to get you to the Sultan's summer residence. So it might interest you to know that we will be travelling there by traditional means.'

At this, Sara's head jerked up in surprise. 'You don't mean an old-fashioned camel caravan?'

Suleiman smiled. 'Indeed I do. A little-used means of desert travel nowadays, but many of the nomadic people still claim it is the most efficient.'

'And who's to say they aren't right? Gosh, I haven't been on one since I was a child.' Sara looked at him, her violet eyes shining with excitement. 'And of course, this means that there will be horses, too.'

Suleiman felt his throat tighten. Was it wrong that he found the look on her face utterly captivating? That her smile would have warmed a tent on the coldest desert night. 'I had forgotten how much you enjoyed riding,' he said.

'Well, you shouldn't—because it's thanks to you that I ride so well.'

'You were an exemplary pupil,' he said gruffly.

She inclined her head, as if she was acknowledging the sudden cessation in hostilities between them. 'Thank you. But your lessons were what gave me my confidence and my ability.'

'Do you still ride?'

She shook her head. 'There aren't too many stables in the middle of London.' She looked at him. 'But I miss it.'

Something about the vulnerable pout of her lips made him ask the indulgent question, despite his own silent protestations that their conversation was becoming much too intimate. 'And what do you miss about it?'

She wriggled her shoulders. 'It's the time when I feel most free, I guess.'

Their eyes met and Suleiman saw a sudden shadow cross her face. It was almost as if she'd just remembered something—something which made her face take on a new and determined expression.

He watched as she smoothed down the silk of her blouse, her fingers whispering over the delicate material which covered her ribcage. Why did she insist on doing that, he wondered furiously—when all it was doing was making him focus on her body? And he must *stop* thinking of her body. And her violet eyes. He must think of her only as the woman who would soon be married to the Sultan—the man for whom he would lay down his life.

'We're nearly there,' he said, his sudden lust tempered by relief as the powerful jet began its descent.

Their arrival at the airbase had been kept deliberately low-key, since all celebrations had been put on hold until the wedding. Suleiman watched the natural grace with which Sara walked down the aircraft steps and then moved along the small line of officials who were assembled to meet her. She had lowered her lashes to a demure level, in order to conceal the brilliant gleam of her eyes, and her lips were curved into a serene and highly appropriate little smile. She could easily become an exemplary Sultana, he thought, despising himself for the dull ache of disappointment which followed this thought.

Afterwards, he watched her look around her, as if she was reacquainting herself with the vastness and beauty of the desert. He saw the admiration in her eyes as she gazed up at the mighty herd of camels standing at the edge of the airstrip, where the land was always waiting to encroach. And wasn't she only reflecting his own feelings about this particular form of transport?

A camel caravan could consist of a hundred and fifty animals, but since this endeavour was mainly ceremonial there were no more than eighteen beasts. Some were topped with lavishly fringed tents while others carried necessary provisions for the journey. Men on horseback moved up and down the line, riding some of the finest Akhal-Teke horses in the world, their distinctive coats gleaming metallic in the bright sun.

'It's pretty spectacular, isn't it?' he observed.

'It's more than that. I think it's one of the most beautiful sights in the world,' she said softly.

He turned to her and suddenly he didn't care if he was breaking protocol in the eyes of the onlookers. Wasn't this his opportunity to make amends for having let his lust override his duty to the Sultan, on the night of her brother's coronation? Couldn't he say the *right* thing to her now? The thing she needed to hear, rather than the impure thoughts which were still making him hard whenever he was near her.

'That is genuine passion I hear in your voice, Sara,' he said. 'Can't you piece together the many things you love about the desert? Then you could flick through them as you would a precious photo album—and be grateful for the many beauties of the life which will be yours when you marry.'

'But they won't be mine, will they?' she demanded. 'Everything will belong to my husband—including me! Because we both know that, by law, women in Qurhah are not allowed ownership of anything. I'll just be there, some bored figurehead, sitting robed and trapped. Free only to communicate with my husband and my female servants—apart from at official functions, and even then the guests to whom I will be introduced will be highly vetted. I don't know how the Sultan's sister stands it.'

'The Princess Leila is deeply contented in her royal role,' said Suleiman.

Sara closed her lips together. That wasn't what she'd heard. Apparently, at the famous Qurhah Gold Cup races,

Leila had been seen looking glum—but it was hardly her place to drop the princess in it.

'I'll probably have to fight to be able to ride a horse,' she continued. 'And only when any stray man has been cleared away from the scene in case he dares *look* at me. *And* I'll probably be forced to ride side-saddle.'

'You do not have to be bored,' he argued. 'Boredom is simply a question of attitude. You could use your good fortune and good health to make Qurhah a better place. You could do important work for charity.'

'That goes without saying,' she said. 'I'm more than happy to do that. But am I to be consigned to a loveless marriage, simply because my country got itself into debt?'

Suleiman felt a terrible conflict raging within him. The conflict of believing what was right and knowing what was wrong. The conflict of duty versus desire. He wanted nothing more than to rescue her from her fate. To tell her that she need not marry a man she did not love. And then to drag her off to some dark corner and slide those silken robes from her lush young body. He wanted to rub the nub of his thumb between her legs, to feel the moist flowering of her sex as her body prepared itself for his entry. He wanted to bite at her breasts. To leave the dark indentation of his teeth behind. His mark. So that no other man would be able to touch her...

With an effort he closed his mind to the torture of his erotic thoughts—for that way lay madness. He could do nothing other than what he had promised to do. He would deliver Sara to the Sultan and he would forget her, just as he had forgotten every woman he had ever lain with.

'This is your destiny,' he breathed. 'And you cannot escape it.'

'No?'

He watched, fascinated and appalled as the rosy tip of her tongue emerged from her lips and began to trace a featherlight path around their cupid's bow. And suddenly all he could think about was the exquisite gleam of those lips.

'You can't think of any alternative solution to my dilemma?' she questioned softly.

For a moment he thought of entering eagerly into the madness which was nudging at the edges of his mind. Of telling her that the two of them would fly away and he would spend the rest of his life protecting her and making love to her. That they would create a future together with children of their own. And they would build the kind of home that neither of them had ever known.

He shook his head, as if emerging from an unexpected dream.

'The solution to your *dilemma*,' he said coldly, 'is to shake off your feelings of self-pity—and start counting your blessings instead. Be grateful that you will soon be the wife of His Imperial Majesty. And now, let us join the caravan and begin our journey—for the Sultan grows impatient. You will take the second camel in the train.'

'I will not,' she said.

'I beg your pardon?'

'You heard—and glaring at me like that won't make any difference, Suleiman,' she said. 'I want to ride one of those beautiful horses.'

'You will not be riding anywhere.'

'Oh, but I will,' she argued stubbornly. 'Because either you let me have my own mount, or I'll refuse to get on one of the camels—and I'd like to see any of you trying to get a woman on top of a camel if she doesn't want to go. Apart from the glaring problem of propriety—I have a very healthy pair of lungs and I doubt whether screaming is considered appropriate behaviour for a princess. You know how much the servants gossip.'

Suleiman could feel a growing frustration as he acknowledged the fierce look on her face. 'Are you calling my bluff?' he demanded.

'No. I'm just telling you that I don't intend to spend the next three days sitting on a camel. I get travel-sick on camels—you know that!'

'You have been allocated the strongest and yet most docile beast in the caravan,' he defended.

'I don't care if he's fluent in seven languages—I'm not getting on him. Please, Suleiman,' she coaxed. 'Let me ride. I've got my eye on that sweet-looking palomino over there.'

'But you told me you haven't been on a horse for years,' he growled.

'I know. And that's precisely why I need the practice. So either you let me ride there, or I shall refuse to come.'

He met her obstinate expression, knowing she had him beat. Imagine the dishonour to her reputation if he tried to force her onto the back of a camel. 'If I agree—*if* I agree...you will stay close beside me at all times!' he ordered.

'If you insist.'

'I do. And you will not do anything reckless. Is that understood?'

'Perfectly,' she said.

Frustratedly, he shook his head—wondering how the Sultan was going to be able to cope with such a *headstrong* woman.

But a far more pressing problem was how he was going to get through the next couple of days without succumbing to the temptation of making love to her.

CHAPTER FOUR

SARA GAVE A small sigh of satisfaction as she submitted to the ministrations of the female attendant. Luxuriously, she wriggled her toes and rested her head against the back of the small bath tub. It was strange being waited on like this again after so long. On the plane she had decided she didn't like being treated like a princess, but that wasn't quite true. Because nobody could deny that it felt wonderful to have your body washed in cool water, especially when you had been on horseback all day beneath the baking heat of the desert sun.

They had spent hours travelling across the Mekathasinian Sands towards the Sultan's summer palace and until a few moments ago she had been hot and tired. But according to Suleiman they had made good progress—and hadn't it felt wonderful to be back in the saddle again after so long?

She had stubbornly ignored his suggestion that she ride side-saddle. Instead, she had lightly swung up onto her beautiful Akhal-Teke mount with its distinctive metallic golden coat, before going for a gentle trot with the black-eyed emissary close by. When she'd been going for a couple of hours, he had grudgingly agreed to let her canter. She suspected that he was testing her competence in the saddle and she must have passed the test—for it had taken very little persuasion for him to agree to a short gallop with her across the desert plain.

And that bit. That bit had been bliss…

She closed her eyes as the cool water washed away the sand which still clung to her skin. Today had been one of the best days she could remember—and how crazy was that? Shouldn't pleasure be the last thing which a woman in her position should be feeling?

Yet the freedom of riding with Suleiman beneath the hot desert sun had been powerful enough to make her forget that she was getting ever closer to a destiny which filled her with horror.

It had felt fantastic to be back on a horse again. She had eagerly agreed to his offer of a race, although at one point she'd been lagging behind him as they were galloping towards the sand dune. Suleiman had turned to look at her and had slowed his horse to match her pace.

'Are you okay, Sara? Not feeling too tired?'

'Oh, I'm okay.' Without warning, she had dug her knees into the horse and had surged ahead. And of course she reached the dune first—laughing at the frustration and admiration which were warring in his dark eyes.

'You little cheat,' he murmured.

'It's called tactics, Suleiman.' Her answer had been insouciant, but she had been unable to hide her instinctive glee at having beaten him. 'Just plain old tactics.'

It was only now, with the relaxation which followed hours of physical exertion, that her thoughts were slowing down enough to let her dwell on the inevitable.

One day down and time was ticking away. Soon she would never be alone with him again.

The thought of that was hard to bear. Within a few short hours, all those feelings she'd repressed for so long had come flooding back with all the force of a burst dam. He was the only man she'd ever felt anything for and he still was. She couldn't believe how badly she had underestimated the impact of being in his company again.

She had been planning to use him as her means of escape, yes. What she hadn't been planning was to fall deeper under his spell. To imagine herself still in love with him, as she'd been all those years ago. Had she forgotten the power of the heart to yearn for the impossible? Or had she just forgotten that Suleiman was her fantasy man, who had now come to vibrant life before her eyes?

On horseback, he looked like a dream. He had changed into his desert clothes and the result had been breathtaking. Sara had forgotten how good a man could look in flowing robes and had spent most of the day trying not to stare at him, with varying degrees of success. The fluid fabric had clung to his body and moulded the powerful thrust of his thighs as they'd gripped the flanks of his stallion. His headdress had streamed behind him like a pale banner in the warm air. His rugged profile had been dark and commanding—his lips firmly closed against the clouds of fine sand which billowed up around him.

She lay back as the servant continued to wash her with a mixture of rose water, infused with jasmine blossom. Next, her ears would be anointed with oil of sandalwood, a process which would be repeated on her toes. After that, her hair would be woven with fragrant leaves which had been brought from the gardens of the Sultan's palace and the intention was for her to be completely perfumed by the time she was presented to him at court.

Sara shuddered as she imagined the swarthy potentate stripping her of her bridal finery, before lowering his powerful body on hers.

She could not go through with it.

She would not go through with it.

For the Sultan's sake and for all their sakes—she could not become his wife.

And deep down she knew that the only way to ensure her freedom was with the seduction of Suleiman.

Yet the nagging question remained about how she was going to accomplish that. How could such a scenario be possible when silent servants hovered within the shadows of the camels and the tents? When the eyes of the bodyguards were so sharp it was said they could see a snake move from a hundred yards away.

The light was fading by the time she emerged from the tasselled tent for the evening meal. Against the clear, cobalt sky the giant desert sun looked like a fiery giant beach-ball as it sank slowly into the horizon. She found herself remembering the week she'd spent in

Ibiza last year—when, bikini-clad, she'd frolicked in the waves with two girlfriends from the office, enjoying the kind of freedom she'd only ever dreamed of. Would she ever do something like that again? Would she ever be able to wander down to the deli near Gabe's offices and buy herself a cappuccino, with an extra shot?

Her silken robes fluttered in the gentle breeze and tiny silver bells adorned the jewellery she wore. They jangled at her wrists and her ankles as she moved—and apart from their decorative qualities, that was the whole point of wearing them—to warn others that the Sultan's fiancée was in the vicinity. As soon as the sound was heard the servants would bow their heads and the male members of the group would quickly avert their eyes.

All except Suleiman.

He had been standing talking to one of the bodyguards but he must have heard her for he glanced up, his eyes narrowing. It was impossible to know what was on his mind but she knew she hadn't imagined the sudden tension which had stiffened his body. She saw his mouth harden and the skin stretching tautly over his cheekbones—as if he was mentally preparing himself for some sort of endurance test.

The bodyguards had melted away into the shadows and even though the temporary camp was humming with the unseen life of servants, it felt as if it were just her and him, alone beneath the vast canopy of the darkening sky, which would soon give way to starry night.

He, too, had changed for dinner. Soft robes of dark crimson silk made him look as if he were part of the setting sun himself. His ebony hair was covered with a headdress which was held in place by a woven circlet of silver cord. There was no aristocratic blood in his veins—that much she knew about a childhood of which he rarely spoke—but at that moment he looked as proud and patrician as any king.

He bowed his head as she approached, but not quickly enough to hide the sudden flash of hunger in his eyes.

'You look like a true desert princess tonight,' he said.

'I can't make up my mind whether or not that's a compliment.'

'It is,' he said, looking for all the world as if he now regretted his choice of words. 'It signals that you are accepting your fate—outwardly, at least. Are you hungry?'

She nodded. The sight of Suleiman was enough to make food seem inconsequential, but she could smell cooking. The familiar concoction of sweet herbs and spices drifting towards her was making her mouth water and it was a long time since she had eaten a feast in the desert. 'Starving.'

He laughed. 'Don't they say that a hungry woman is a dangerous woman?'

'And don't they also say that some women remain dangerous even when their bellies are full?'

'Is that a threat or a promise?'

She looked into his eyes. So black, she thought. So very black. 'Which would you like it to be, Suleiman?'

There was a split second of a pause, when she

thought he might respond in a similar, teasing style. But then something about his countenance changed and his face darkened. She could see him swallow—as if something jagged had lodged itself in his throat. And was it a terrible thing to admit that she found herself almost *enjoying* his obvious discomfort?

Well, it might be terrible, but it was also human nature—and right now, nothing else seemed to matter. She was achingly aware that beneath their supposedly polite banter thrummed the unmistakable tremor of sexual desire. She wanted to break down the walls that he had built around himself—to claw away at the bricks with her bare hands. She wanted to seduce him to guarantee her freedom, yes—but it was more than that. Because she wanted him.

She had never stopped wanting him.

But this could never be anything more than sex. She knew that. If she seduced Suleiman, then she needed to have the strength to walk away. Because no happy ending was possible. She knew that, too.

'It's dinner time,' he said abruptly, glancing at the sun, which she knew he could read as accurately as any clock.

Sara said nothing as they walked over to the campfire, where a special dining area had been laid out for the two of them. She saw the fleeting disquiet which had darkened Suleiman's face and realised that this faux-intimacy was probably the last thing he wanted. But protocol being what it was—there was really no alternative. Of course she would be expected to eat with him, rather than alone—while the servants ate their own rations out of sight.

It was a long time since she had enjoyed a meal in the desert and, inevitably, the experience had a storybook feel to it. The giant bulk of the camels was silhouetted against the darkening sky, where the first stars were beginning to glimmer. The crackling flames glowed golden and the smell of the traditional Qurhah stew was rich with the scent of oranges and cinnamon.

Sara sank down onto a pile of brocade cushions while Suleiman adopted a position on the opposite side of the low table, on which thick, creamy candles burned. It was as if an outdoor dining room had been erected in the middle of the sands and it looked spectacular. She'd forgotten how much could be loaded onto the backs of the camels and how it was a Qurhah custom to make every desert trip feel like a home-from-home.

She accepted a beaker of pomegranate juice and smiled her thanks at the servant who ladled out a portion of the stew onto each of the silver platters, before leaving the two of them alone.

The food was delicious and Sara ate several mouthfuls but her hunger soon began to ebb away. It was too distracting to think about eating when Suleiman was sitting opposite her, his face growing shadowed in the dying light. She noticed he was watching her closely—his intelligent eyes narrowed and gleaming—and she knew that she must approach this very carefully. He could not be played with and toyed with. If she went about her proposed seduction in a crass and obvious manner, then mightn't he see through it?

So try to get underneath his skin—without him realising what you're doing.

'You do realise that I've known you for years and yet you're still something of a mystery to me,' she said conversationally.

'Good. That's the way I like it.'

'I mean, I know practically nothing about your past,' she continued, as if he hadn't made that terse interruption.

'How many times have I told you, Sara? My past is irrelevant.'

'I don't agree. Surely our past is what defines us. It makes us what we are today. And you've never told me how you first got to know the Sultan—or to be regarded so highly by him. When I was a child you said I wouldn't understand—and when I became an adult, well...' She shrugged, not wanting to spell it out. Not needing to say that once sexual attraction had reared its powerful head, any kind of intimacy had seemed too dangerous. She put her fork down and looked at him.

'It isn't relevant,' he said.

'Well, what else are we going to talk about? And if I am to be the Sultan's wife...' She hesitated as she noticed him flinch. 'Then surely it must be relevant. Am I to know nothing about the background of the man who was my future husband's aide for so long? You must admit that it is highly unusual for such a powerful man as the Sultan to entrust so much to someone who has no aristocratic blood of their own.'

'I had no idea that you were such a snob, Sara,' he mocked.

'I'm not a snob,' she corrected. 'Just someone seeking the facts. That's one of the side effects of having had a western education. I was taught to question things, rather than just to accept what I was told or be fobbed off with some bland reply designed to put me in my place.'

'Then maybe your western education has not served you well,' he said, before suddenly stilling. He shook his head. 'What am I saying?' he said, almost to himself. 'How unforgivable of me to try to damn your education and in so doing—to damn knowledge itself. Forget that I ever said that.'

'Does that mean you'll answer my question?'

'That is not what I meant at all.'

'Please, Suleiman.'

He gave an exasperated sigh as he looked at her. But she thought she saw affection in his eyes too as he lowered his voice and began to speak in English, even though Sara was certain that none of the servants or bodyguards were within earshot.

'You know that I was born into poverty?' he said. 'Real and abject poverty?'

'I heard the rumours,' Sara answered. 'Though you'd never guess that from your general bearing and manner.'

'I learn very quickly. Adaption is the first lesson of survival,' he said drily. 'And believe me, it's easier to absorb the behaviour of the rich, than it is the other way round.'

'So how did you—a boy from the wrong side of the tracks—ever come into contact with someone as important as the Sultan?'

There was silence for a moment. Sara thought she saw a sudden darkness cross his face. And there was bitterness, too.

'I grew up in a place called Tymahan, a small area of Samahan, where the land is at its most desolate and people eke out what living they can. To be honest, there was never much of a living to be made—even before the last war, when much blood was shed. But you, of course—in your pampered palace in Dhi'ban—would have known nothing of those hardships.'

'You cannot blame me for the way I was protected as a princess,' she protested. 'Would you sooner I had cut off my hair and pretended to be a boy, in order to do battle?'

'No.' He shook his head. 'Of course not.'

'Carry on with your story,' she urged, leaning forward a little.

He seemed to draw in a quick breath as she grew closer.

'The Sultan's father was touring the region,' he said. 'He wanted to witness the aftermath of the wars and to see whether any insurrection remained.'

Sara watched as he took a sip from his beaker and then put the drink back down on the low table.

'My mother had been ill—and grieving,' he continued. 'My father had been killed in the uprisings and as a consequence she was vulnerable—struck down by a scourge known to many at that time.' His mouth twisted with pain and bitterness. 'A scourge known as starvation.'

Sara flinched as guilt suddenly washed over her. Earlier, he had accused her of self-pity and didn't he have a point? She had moaned about her position as a princess—yet despite the many unsatisfactory areas of her life, she had certainly never experienced anything as fundamental as a lack of food. She'd never had to face a problem as pressing as basic *survival*. She looked into his black eyes, which were now clouded with pain, and her heart went out to him.

'Oh, Suleiman,' she said softly.

His mouth hardened, as if her sympathy was unwelcome. 'The Sultan was being entertained by a group of local dignitaries and there was enough food groaning on those tables to feed our village for a month,' he said, his voice growing harsh. 'I was lurking in the shadows, for that was my particular skill—to see and yet not be seen. And on this night I saw a pomegranate— as big as a man's fist and as golden as the midday sun. My mother had always loved pomegranates and I...'

'You stole it?' she guessed as his words faded away.

He gave her a tight smile. 'If I had been old enough to articulate my thoughts I would have called it a fair distribution of goods, but my motives were irrelevant since I was caught, red-handed. I may have been good at hiding in the shadows, but I was no match for the Sultan's elite bodyguards.'

Sara shivered, recognising the magnitude of such a crime and wondering how he was still alive to tell the tale.

'And they let you off?'

He gave a short laugh. 'The Sultan's guards are not in the habit of granting clemency to common thieves and I was moments away from losing my head to one of their scimitars, when I saw a young boy about the same age as me running from within one of the royal tents and shouting at them to stop. It was the Sultan's son, Murat.' He paused. 'Your future husband.'

Sara flinched, for she knew that his heavy reminder had been deliberate. 'And what did he do?'

'He saved my life.'

She stared at him in bewilderment. 'How?'

'It was simple. Murat was protected and pampered—but lonely and bored. He wanted a playmate—and a boy hungry enough to steal from the royal table was deemed a charitable cause to rescue. My mother was offered a large sum of money—'

'She took it?'

'She had no choice other than to take it!' he snapped. 'I was to be washed and dressed in fine clothes. To be removed from my own country and taken back to the royal palace of Qurhah, where I was to be educated alongside the young Sultan. In most things, we two boys would be as equals.'

There was silence while she digested this. She could see how completely Suleiman's life would have been transformed. Why sometimes he unconsciously acted with the arrogance known to all royals, though his was tempered by a certain *edge*. But his mother had *sold* him. And there was something he had omitted to mention. 'Your...mother? What happened to her?'

This time the twist of pain on his face was so raw that she could hardly bear to observe it.

'She was given the best food and the best medicines,' he said. 'And a new dwelling place was built for her and my two younger brothers. I was taken away to the palace, intending to return to Samahan to see my family in the summer. But her illness had taken an irreversible toll and my mother died that springtime. I never...I never saw her again.'

'Oh, Suleiman,' she said, her heart going out to him. His mother's sacrifice had been phenomenal and yet she had died without seeing her eldest son. How terrible for them both. She wanted to go to him and take him in her arms, but the unseen presence of the servants and the expression on his face warned her not to try. Only words could convey her empathy and her sorrow and she picked the simplest and most heartfelt of all. 'I'm sorry,' she said. 'So very sorry.'

'It happened a long time ago,' he said harshly. 'It's all in the past. And that's where it should stay. Like I said, the past is irrelevant. Now perhaps you will understand why I prefer not to talk of it?'

She looked at him. All these years she'd known him—or, rather, had thought she'd known him. But she had only seen the bits he had allowed her to see. He had kept this vital part of himself locked away, until now—when it had poured from his lips and made him seem strangely vulnerable. It made her understand a little more about why he was the kind of man he was. Why he kept his feelings bottled away and sometimes seemed so stubborn and inflexible. It explained why he had always been so unquestioningly loyal to the Sultan who had saved his life. He was so driven by duty—because duty was all he knew.

Suddenly she realised why he had rejected her on the night of her brother's coronation. Again, because it was his *duty*. Because she had been betrothed to the Sultan.

Yet the price of duty had been to never see his mother again. No wonder he had always seemed so proud and so alone. Because essentially he was.

And suddenly Sara knew that she could not seduce him as some cynical game-plan of her own. She could not use Suleiman Abd al-Aziz to help her escape from this particular prison. She could not place him in any position of danger, because if the Sultan were ever to discover that his bride-to-be had slept with the man he most trusted in all the world—then all hell would be let loose.

No. She lifted her hand to brush a strand of hair away from her cheek and she saw his eyes narrow as the bells on her silver bangles tinkled. She was going to have to be strong and take responsibility for herself.

She could not use sex as an instrument of barter, not when she cared about Suleiman so much. If she wanted to get out of here, then she was going to have to use more traditional means. But she was resourceful, wasn't she? There was nothing stopping her.

She needed to make her bid for freedom without implicating Suleiman. Even if he was blamed for her departure, he should not be party to it. Somehow she needed to escape without him knowing—and escape she would. She would return to the military airfield and *demand* to be put on a plane back to England—promising them a sure-fire international outcry if they failed to comply with her wishes. They kept wanting to remind her that she was a princess—well, maybe it was time she started behaving like one!

She rose to her feet but Suleiman was shadowing her every move and was by her side in an instant.

'I must turn in for the night,' she said, giving a huge yawn and wondering if it looked as staged as it felt. 'The effects of the desert heat are very wearying and I'm no longer used to it.'

He inclined his head. 'Very well. Then I accompany you to your tent.'

'There's no need for you to do that.'

'There is every need, Sara—for we both know that snakes and scorpions can lurk within the shadows.'

She wanted to tell him that she knew the terrain as well as he did. That she had been taught to understand and respect its mysteries and its dangers, because he had taught them to her. But perhaps now was not a good time to remind him that at heart she was a child of the desert—for mightn't that alert him to all the possibilities which still lay beneath her fingertips?

The beauty of the night seemed to mock her. The sky was a vast dark dome, pinpricked by the brightest stars a person was ever likely to see. The moon brightened the indigo depths like a giant silver dish which had been superimposed there—the shadows on its face disturbingly clear. For a moment she wished that she had supernatural powers—that she could leap into the air and fly to the moon, like the most famous of all the Dhi'banese fables she had heard as a child.

But her sandaled feet were firmly on the ground as she walked through the soft sand, her eyes taking in her surroundings. She looked at the layout of the camp as she walked. She saw where the horses were tethered and where the bodyguards had been stationed. Obviously they were close enough to keep her from harm, but far enough away for propriety to be observed.

They reached the tasselled entrance of her tent and she wanted to reach up and touch Suleiman's face, aware that the sands of time were running out for them. If she could have just one wish, it would be to run her fingers through the thick ebony of his hair and then to kiss him. But nothing more. She'd changed her mind about that. She suspected that to have sex with him would rob her of all the strength she possessed, and leave her yearning for him for the rest of her life. Perhaps it was best all round that making love was an option which was no longer open to her. But oh, to be able to kiss him...

Would it be so very wrong to bid him goodnight, as she had done to male friends in England countless times before?

On impulse, she rose on tiptoe and brushed her lips over first one of his cheeks, and then the other. It could not have been misinterpreted by anyone. Even the Sultan—if he had been standing there—would have recognised it as a very unthreatening form of western greeting, or farewell. He might not have liked it, but he would have understood it.

Except that this time, that quick brush of her lips was threatening her very sanity. She could feel the hammering of her heart and the hot flush of colour to her face. She could feel the whisper of her breath on his cheeks as she kissed each one in turn. And she could hear, too, the startled intake of breath he took in response. It should have been innocent and yet it felt light years from innocence. How could that be? How could one innocuous touch feel so powerful that it seemed to have rocked her to the core of her being?

Their eyes met and clashed in the indigo light as silent messages of desire and need passed between them. Her skin screamed out for him to touch it. The thrum of sexual tension was now so loud that it almost deafened her.

Slowly, his gaze travelled from her face, all the way down her lavishly embroidered gown, until it lingered at last on the swell of her bodice. The sensation of him looking so openly at her breasts was so *exciting*. It was making her nipples prickle with hunger and frustration. She sucked in an unsteady breath which made her chest rise and fall, and she heard him utter a soft groan.

For a moment he seemed about to move towards her and she prayed that he would. Kiss me, she prayed silently. Just kiss me one more time and I will never ask again.

But the suggestion of movement was arrested as quickly as it had begun for suddenly he stiffened, his face hardening into a granite-like mask. His eyes deadened into dull ebony and when he spoke, his voice was ragged and tinged with self-disgust.

'Get to bed, Sara,' he bit out harshly. 'For God's sake, just get to bed.'

CHAPTER FIVE

SARA AWOKE EARLY. Before even the early light they called the 'false dawn' had begun to brighten the arid desert landscape outside her tent. She lay there in the silence for a moment or two, collecting her thoughts and wondering whether she had the nerve to go through with her plan. But then she thought about reality. About needing to get away from Suleiman just as badly as she needed to get away from her forced marriage to the Sultan.

She had no choice.

She *had* to escape.

Silently, she slipped from beneath the covers of her bedding, still wearing the clothes she had slept in all night. Just before dismissing the servant last evening, she had asked one of them to bring her a large water-bottle as well as a tray of mint tea and a bowl of sugar cubes. The girl had looked a little surprised but had done as requested—no doubt putting Sara's odd request down to the vagaries of being a princess.

Now she wrapped a soft, silken veil around her head before peeping out from behind the flaps of the tent, and her heart lifted with relief. All was quiet. Not a soul around. She glanced upwards at the sky. It looked clear enough. Soon it would be properly light and with light came danger. The animals would grow restless and all the bodyguards would waken. She cocked her head as she heard a faint but unmistakable noise. Did that mean one of the guards was already awake? Her heart began to pound. She must be off, with not a second more to be wasted.

Stealthily, she moved across the sand to where the horses were tethered. The Akhal-Teke palomino she had been riding earlier greeted her with a soft whinny and she shushed him by feeding him a sugar cube, which he crunched eagerly with his big teeth. Her heart was thumping as she mounted him and then urged him forward on a walk going with the direction of the wind, not giving him his head and letting him gallop until they were well out of earshot of the campsite.

Her first feelings were of exhilaration and delight that she had got away without being seen. That she had escaped the dark-eyed scrutiny of Suleiman and had not implicated him in her flight. The pale sky was becoming bluer by the second and the sand was a pleasing shade of deep gold. Suddenly, this felt like an adventure and her life in London seemed a long way away.

She made good progress before the sun grew too high, when she stopped beside a rock to relieve herself and then to drink sparingly from her water bottle. When she remounted her horse it was noticeably hotter and she was glad of the veil which shielded her head from the increasingly strong rays. And at least the camel trail was easy enough to follow back towards the airbase. The tread of the heavy beasts was deep and there had been none of the threatened sandstorms overnight to sweep away the evidence of their route.

Did she stop paying attention?

Did her ever-present thoughts of Suleiman distract her for long enough to make her stray from the deep line of animal footprints she'd been following so intently?

Was that why one minute she seemed so secure in her direction, while the next…?

Blinking, Sara looked around like someone who had just awoken from a dream, telling herself that the trail was still there if she looked for it and she had probably just wandered a little way from it.

It took only a couple of minutes for her to realise that her self-reassurance was about as real as a mirage.

Because there was nothing. Nothing to be seen.

She blinked again. No indentations. No little tell-tale heaps where a frisky camel might have kicked out at the sand.

Panic rose in her throat like bile but she fought to keep it at bay. Because panicking would not help. Most emphatically it would not. It would make her start to lose her nerve and she couldn't afford to lose anything else—losing her way was bad enough.

She didn't even have a compass with her.

She dismounted from her horse, trying to remember the laws of survival as she took a thirsty gulp of water from her bottle. She should retrace her steps. That was what she should do. Find where she'd lost the path and then pick up the camel trail again. Bending, she lifted a small pebble out of the sand. Sucking it would remind her to keep her mouth closed and prevent it from drying out.

She patted the horse before swinging lightly into the saddle again. It was going to be all right, she told herself. Of course it was going to be all right. It had only been a couple of minutes since she'd missed the path and she couldn't possibly be lost.

It took her about an hour of fruitless riding to accept that she was.

'What do you mean, she's not there?'

His voice distorted with anger, Suleiman stared at the bent head of the female servant who stood trembling before him.

'Tell me!' he raged.

The girl began to babble. They had thought that the princess was sleeping late, so they did not wish to disturb her.

'So you left the princess's tent until now?'

'Y-yes, sir.'

Suleiman forced himself to suck in a deep breath, only just managing to keep his hot rage from erupting as he surveyed the bodyguards who were milling around nervously. 'And not one of you thought to wonder why one of the horses was missing?' he demanded.

But their shamefaced excuses were quelled with a furious wave of his hand as Suleiman marched over to the horses, with the most senior bodyguard close behind him. Because deep down he knew that he was not really in any position to criticise—not when he was as culpable as they.

Why hadn't *he* been watching her?

His mouth hardened as he swung himself up onto the biggest and most powerful stallion.

Because he was a coward, that was why.

Despite his supposedly exemplary military record and all the awards which had been heaped upon him— he had selected a tent as far away from hers as possible. Too unsure of his reaction to her proximity, he had not dared risk being close. Not trusting himself—and not trusting her either.

He hadn't imagined the white-hot feeling of lust which had flared between them last night and he was too experienced a lover to mistake the look of sexual yearning which had darkened her violet eyes. When she was standing in front of him in her embroidered robes—her hair woven with fragrant leaves—he had never wanted her quite so much.

Hadn't he wondered whether her western sensibilities might make her take the initiative? Hadn't he wondered whether she might boldly arrive naked at his tent under cover of darkness and slip into his bed without invitation, as so many women had done before?

He stared down at the senior bodyguard. 'You have checked her trail?'

'Yes, boss. She has headed due north—taking the same path by which we came, back towards the airbase.'

Suleiman nodded. It was as he had thought. She was trying to get back to England on her own—oh, most stubborn and impetuous of women! 'Very well,' he said. 'I will follow her trail. And you will assign three men to take up the other three points of the compass and to set off immediately. But no more than three. I don't want the desert paths disturbed any more than they need be. I don't want any clues churned up by the damned horses.'

'Yes, boss.'

'You will also send someone to find a high enough vantage point to try to get a mobile phone signal. I want the military base informed and I want every damned plane at their disposal out looking for her. Understand?'

The bodyguard nodded. 'Understood.'

'And believe me when I tell you that you have not heard the last of this!'

With his final, angry words ringing Suleiman galloped off at a furious pace, the warm wind streaming against his face as he followed the mixed track of the camels and the newer footprints of Sara's horse.

He had already realised that there would be repercussions. By involving the military, word would inevitably get back to the Sultan that the princess was missing. But he didn't care what criticism or punishment came his way for having lost the future Sultana of Qurhah. They could exile him or imprison him and he wouldn't care.

He didn't care about anything other than finding her safe and well.

He had never known such raw fear as he travelled beneath the heat of a sun which was growing ever more blistering. Even though she was out of practice, he knew that she was a sound horsewoman—a fact which had always been a source of pride since he had been the one to tutor her, but which now gave him only comfort. And he found himself clinging to that one small comfort. Please let her ride safely, he prayed. Please not let something have frightened the horse so that Sara might be lying there buckled and broken on the sand. Alone and scared while the sun beat down on her and the vultures waited to peck out her beautiful violet eyes...

He sucked in a breath of hot air which felt raw as it travelled down his throat. He should not think the worst. He would not think the worst. Think positive, he told himself. At least no snake or brown scorpion could touch her when she was high up on her horse.

But knowing that did not help him locate her, did it?

Where was she? Where *was* she?

His eyes trained unblinkingly on the ground before him—he saw the exact point where her path had veered off from the main route. Had something distracted the horse? Distracted her?

He pushed forward now, letting the powerful stallion stream across the sands until Suleiman urged it to a halt and then opened his mouth to call across the desolate landscape.

'Sara! Sa-ra!'

But the ensuing response was nothing but an empty silence and his heart gave a painful lurch.

He forced himself to take a drink from one of the water-bottles he carried, for dehydration would be good for neither of them if he found her.

When he found her.
He had to find her.

The position of the sun and his wristwatch told him that he had been searching for her for over four hours. He could feel his heart pumping painfully in his chest. The heat of the midday sun was a tough enough combatant but darkness was a whole different ball-game.

He thought of the nocturnal creatures which came out in the cold of the desert night—dangerous animals which populated this inhospitable terrain.

'Sara!' he called again and then the horse's ears pricked up and Suleiman strained to hear a sound that was almost lost in the distance. He listened again.

It *was* a sound. The smallest sound in the world. The sound of a voice. If it had been anyone else's voice, he might not have recognised it—but Suleiman had heard Sara's voice in many guises. He'd heard it as a child. He'd heard its hesitancy in puberty and its breathlessness in passion. But he had never heard it sound quite so broken nor so lost as it did right now.

'Sara!' he yelled, the word spilling from his lips as if it had been ripped from the very base of his lungs.

And then the shout again. Due east a little. He pressed his thighs against the flanks of the horse and urged it forward in a gallop in the direction of the sound. He heard nothing more and as the silence grew, so too did his fear that he had simply imagined it. An aural version of a desert mirage...

Until he saw the shape of a rock up ahead. A dark red rock which soared up revealing a dark cool cave underneath against which gleamed the metallic golden sheen of an Akhal-Teke palomino. He narrowed his eyes, for the horse carried no rider, and he galloped forward to see Sara leaning back against the rock. Its shadow consumed her with its terracotta light but he could see that her face was white with fear and her eyes looked like two deep pools of violet ink.

Grabbing a water-bottle, he jumped from the horse's back and was beside her in a moment. He held the vessel to her lips and she sucked on it greedily, like a small animal being bottle-fed. He put the bottle down and as he watched the colour and the strength return to her all his own fear and anger bubbled up inside him.

'What the hell did you think you were doing?' he demanded, levering her up against him so that her face was inches away from his.

'Isn't it obvious?' Her voice sounded weak. 'I was trying to get away.'

'You could have died!'

'I'm not...I'm not that easy to get rid of,' she said, her lips trying for a smile but he noticed she didn't quite achieve it—though nothing could disguise the flash of relief which flared briefly in her eyes.

'Where were you headed for?' he demanded, watching as he saw her face assume a look of sudden wariness.

She looked at him from the shuttered forest of her lashes. 'Where do you think? Back to the airport.'

'To the military base?'

'Yes, to the military base. To demand to be taken back to England. I...I came to my senses, Suleiman. I realised that I couldn't go through with it after all—

no matter what you or the Sultan threatened me with, I don't care. I don't care about political dynasties or forging an alliance between my country and his. My brother will have to find someone else to offer up as a human sacrifice.'

Furiously, he stood up and pulled out his mobile phone and started barking into it in Qurhahian. Sara could hear him telling the military that the search should be called off. That the princess had been found and she was safely in his charge.

But when he terminated the call the look on his face didn't make Sara feel in the least bit safe. In fact, it made her feel the opposite of safe. His black eyes were filled with fury as he slowly advanced towards her again.

'So let me get this straight,' he said, and she could tell that he was only just holding onto his temper. 'You took off on your own into one of the most hostile territories in the world—even though you have not ridden for years and have been living a pampered life in London—is that right?'

Her gaze was defiant as she met the accusation in his eyes.

'Yes,' she said fiercely. 'That's exactly right.'

The absurdity of her quest infuriated him. He thought about the danger she'd put herself in and he felt the clench of anger—and fear too, at the thought of what could have happened to her. He intended to give her a piece of his mind. To tell her that he felt like putting her across his knee and smacking her. At least, that was what he thought he intended. But somehow it didn't work out like that.

Maybe it was the sight of all that tousled blonde hair, or the violet glitter of her beautiful eyes. Maybe it was because he'd always wanted her and had never stopped wanting her. His desire for her had been like an endless hunger which had eaten him up from the inside out and suddenly there was no controlling it any longer.

He made one last attempt to fight it but his resistance was gone. He'd never felt so powerless in his life as he stared down into her beautiful face and caught hold of her by the shoulders again. Only this time he was pulling her towards him.

'Damn you, Sara,' he whispered. 'Just *damn you.*'

And that was when he started to kiss her.

CHAPTER SIX

SARA GASPED AS Suleiman's mouth drove down on hers. She told herself that this was crazy. That it was only going to lead to heartbreak and tears. She told herself that if she tore herself out of his embrace, then he would let her go. But her body was refusing to listen.

Her body was on fire.

His mouth explored hers and it felt like a dream. Or some hot, X-rated mirage. It surpassed every hope she'd nurtured during these desperate last few hours. Long, grim hours, as she'd realised the full extent of her plight—that she was hopelessly lost in the unforgiving desert. Until the stern-faced emissary had appeared on the empty horizon, astride a gleaming black stallion like her greatest fantasy come true.

And then he had taken the fantasy and given it a sexy embellishment, by pulling her into his arms and giving her this hard and seeking kiss.

Yet this was dangerous, wasn't it? Dangerous for her heart. Dangerous for her soul. She couldn't afford to love this man, no matter how much she wanted him.

She meant to push him away but he pulled her

closer, so that she could smell his raw, male smell. He smelt of sandalwood and salt. The hard sinews of his body were pressed against hers and the proximity of his tight, taut flesh made her want to melt into him. His lips were hard and soft in turn as they kissed her. One minute they were cajoling, the next they were master-fully stating their intent to make love to her.

'Suleiman.' It didn't come out like the protest she intended it to be—it sounded more like a plea.

'Sara,' he said, drawing his mouth away from hers and cupping her face with both his hands. 'Foolish, beautiful, hot-headed Sara.' His gaze raked over her with a mixture of exasperation and lust. 'Why the hell did you take off like that? Why take such a risk?'

'You know why,' she whispered, moving her head fractionally as she sought out another kiss. 'Because I wanted to escape.'

He brushed his lips over hers. Back and forth in a teasing graze. 'Do you still want to escape?'

She nodded her head. 'Yes.'

'Do you?'

She closed her eyes. 'Stop it.'

'I'm waiting for an answer to my question.'

She shook her head. 'N-not any more. At least, not right now. Not if you keep on kissing me like that.'

'That sounds very much like an invitation.' He gave another groan as their mouths meshed together and his breath was warm in her mouth. 'I should put you straight back on that horse and ride you back into camp.'

'Then why are you unbuttoning my tunic?'

'Because I want to taste your nipples.'

'Oh.'

She tipped her head back as his lips trailed a fiery path over her neck, closing her eyes as sensation washed over her. His fingers felt hard and calloused against her delicate flesh. She could feel the slick, wet heat of her sex overwhelming her as he lowered his mouth to trail his tongue over one hardened nipple.

Her mouth grew dry as her lashes fluttered open to watch him. He kissed each breast in turn and then turned his attention to her tunic, peeling it off entirely—along with her slim-fitting trousers. He freed her aching body so that at last her skin was bared to the warm desert air. And to his eyes.

She heard him suck in a ragged breath as he looked down at her and she was glad she was wearing the provocative underwear she'd brought from England. The balcony bra in electric-blue lace and matching thong were both pretty racy, but she'd discovered a while back that she liked wearing expensive lingerie. It had been another aspect of the freedom she'd relished—that she could go into any department store and stock up on X-rated undies and nobody was going to tell her she couldn't.

He said something she couldn't quite make out and the expression in his slitted eyes was suddenly forbidding.

'Is something wrong?' she questioned tentatively.

'Who buys your lingerie for you?' His voice was dark with some unnamed emotion.

'I do.'

'But you buy it for you? Or do you buy it for the men who will enjoy watching you wearing it?' he persisted, slithering his finger inside her thong where she was so wet and so sensitive that she bucked beneath his touch and gave a little cry. His finger stilled. 'Do you?'

Sara nodded, so strung out with pleasure that she barely knew what she was agreeing to. But men liked women to indulge in fantasy, didn't they? She'd read enough erotic literature to know that. Men liked you to pretend to *be* things and to do things. She read that normality was the killer in the bedroom.

Not that they were anywhere near a bedroom, of course—but who cared about that? Why not feed into his fantasies—and her own? Why shouldn't she make love with Suleiman in the wild desert which had spawned her, on this shaded patch of sand? She might not like all the restrictions of life here, but she was sensitive enough to appreciate its beauty. And if Suleiman wanted her to play the femme fatale, then play it she would.

'I'm enjoying wearing it for you,' she answered coyly, her finger moving to trace the curving satin trim of her bra. 'Do you like it?'

He made a sound mid-way between hunger and anger as he pulled off his crimson robes with impatient disregard, until he was also naked. She let her gaze drift over him, her eyes widening as her gaze locked onto the most intimate part of his aroused body—and suddenly she was a little daunted by what she saw.

'Suleiman…' she whispered, but her words faded because he was back in her arms and was touching her again. Moving his hand intimately against her sex and stroking her with pinpoint accuracy. She could smell the scent of her arousal on the air. She could feel the warm rush of blood flooding through her veins. And shouldn't she be touching *him*? She reached down to whisper her fingertips against his silken length, but he stilled her movement by the abrupt clamp of his hand around her wrist.

'No,' he said.

She looked into his eyes, confused. 'Why not?'

'Because I'm too close to coming, that's why. And I want to come when I'm inside you. I want to watch your face as I enter and hear the sounds you make when I move inside you.'

It was the most erotic thing she'd ever heard. Sara swallowed. Suleiman deep inside the one place where she had always longed for him to be. She could feel her skin burning as he spread his robes down on the shaded sand, like a silken blanket for them to lie on. His face was dark and taut as he peeled off her electric-blue underwear, until she lay before him like a naked sacrifice.

She could see the hardness of his erection and the dark whorls of hair from which it sprang. His olive skin gleamed softly in the terracotta light and his dark eyes were as black as tar as he reached for her, bending his lips to hers. The kiss which followed made her gasp with pleasure. It seemed to unlock something deep within her, but when he lifted his head she could see that his eyes were dark with pain.

'My greatest fantasy and my greatest sin,' he said, his voice shaking. 'And it is wrong. We both know that.'

Suddenly Sara was terrified he was going to stop. That she would never know what it was like to have Suleiman Abd al-Aziz make love to her. And she couldn't bear it. She thought she could pretty much bear anything else, but not that. Not now.

Her hand reached up to touch the blackness of his hair, letting her fingers slide beneath the silken strands. 'How can it possibly be wrong, when it feels so right?'

'Don't ask disingenuous questions, Sara. And don't look at me with those big violet eyes, a colour which I've never seen on any woman other than you. Just stop me from doing this. Stop me before it goes any further because I don't have the strength to stop myself.'

'I *can't*,' she whispered. 'Because I…' She nearly said *I love you*, but just in time she bit back the words. 'Because I've wanted this for so long. We both want it. You know that. Please, Suleiman. Make love to me.'

He tilted up her chin and gazed down at her. 'Oh, Sara,' he said, saying her name like an unwilling surrender.

He entered her slowly. So slowly that she thought she would die with the pleasure. She cried out as he made that first thrust—a cry which was disbelieving and exultant.

Suleiman was inside her.

Suleiman was filling her.

Suleiman was…

He groaned as he found his rhythm, moving deeper with each stroke. And Sara suddenly felt as if she had been born for this moment. She wrapped her legs around his back as he splayed his hands over her bare buttocks to drive even deeper. Her breath was coming in shuddered little gasps as he moved inside her. She'd had sex before, but never like this. *Never like this.* It was like everyone said it should be. It was...

And then she stopped thinking. Stopped everything except listening to the demands of her body and letting the pleasure pile on, layer by sensual layer.

She felt it build—desperately sweet, yet tantalisingly elusive. She felt the warmth flood through her as Suleiman's movements became more urgent and she was so locked into his passionate kiss that the first spasms of her orgasm took her almost by surprise. Like a feather which had been lifted by a storm and then tossed around by it, she just went with the flow. She cried out his name as his own body suddenly tensed, and he shuddered violently as he came.

But it was over all too quickly. Abruptly, he pulled out of her—so that all she was aware of was a warmth spurting over her belly. He had *withdrawn* from her! It took a couple of disconcerting moments before she felt together enough to open her eyes and to look at him and when she did she felt almost *embarrassed.* As if the sudden ending had wiped out the magic of what had gone before.

'Why...why did you do that?'

His voice was flat. 'I realised that in our haste to consummate our lust, we hadn't even discussed contraception.'

Sara did her best not to flinch, but it seemed a particularly emotionless thing to say in view of what had just happened. Consummate their *lust*? Was that it? 'I suppose we didn't.'

'Are you on the pill?'

She shook her head. 'No.'

'So we add a baby into the equation and make the situation a million times worse than it already is,' he said bitterly. 'Is that what you wanted?'

She flushed, knowing he was right—and wasn't it the most appalling thing that she found herself wishing that he *had* made her pregnant? How weird was it that some primitive part of her was wishing that Suleiman had planted his seed inside her belly. So that now there would be a baby growing beneath her heart. *His* baby. 'No, of course it wasn't what I wanted.' She met his eyes. 'Why are you being like this?'

'Like what?'

'So...*cold.*'

'Why do you think? Because I've just betrayed the man who saved my life. Because I've behaved like the worst kind of friend.' His gaze swept over her and somehow she knew what he was going to say, almost before the words had left his lips. 'And you weren't even a virgin.'

It was the 'even' which made it worse. As if she'd been nothing but a poor consolation prize. 'Were you expecting me to be?'

'Yes,' he bit out. 'Of course I was!'

'I'm twenty-three years old, Suleiman. I've been living an independent life in London. What did you expect?'

'But you were brought up as a desert princess! To respect your body and cherish your maidenhood. To save your purity for your bridegroom. Your royal bridegroom.' He shook his head. 'Oh, I know you spoke freely of sex and that beneath your clothes you were wearing the kind of lingerie which only a truly liberated woman would wear. But even though I had my suspicions, deep down I thought you remained untouched!'

'Even though you had your suspicions?' she repeated, in disbelief. 'What are you now—some sort of detective?'

'You are destined to be a royal bride,' he flared back. 'And your virginity was an essential part of that agreement. Or at least, that's what I thought.'

'No, Suleiman, that's where you're wrong.' Sitting up, she angrily brushed a heavy spill of hair away from her flushed face. 'You don't think—you just *react*. You don't see me as an individual with my own unique history. You didn't stop to think that I might have desires and needs of my own, just as you do—and presumably just as Murat does. You simply see me as a stereotype. You see what I am *supposed* to be and what I am *supposed* to stand for. The virgin princess who has been bought for the Sultan. Only I am not that person and I will never be!'

'And didn't it occur to you to have made some attempt to communicate your thoughts with the Sultan, *before* he was forced to take matters into his own hand?' Suleiman demanded. 'Didn't it occur to you that running away just wasn't the answer? But you've spent your whole life running away, haven't you, Sara?'

'And you've spent your whole life denying your feelings!'

'I have never denied that!' he flared back. 'It's a pity that more people don't stop neurotically asking themselves whether or not they are "happy"—and just get out there and *do* something instead!'

'Like you've just done, you mean?' she challenged. 'What, did you think to yourself? "Now, how can I punish the princess for running off? I know—I'll seduce her!"'

For a moment there was nothing other than the sound of them struggling to control their breathing and Suleiman felt the cold coil of anger twisting at his gut as he looked at her.

He swallowed but the action did little to ease the burning sensation which scorched his throat. The acrid taste of guilt couldn't be washed away so easily, he thought bitterly.

He had just seduced the woman who was to marry the Sultan.

He had just committed the ultimate betrayal against his sovereign—and wasn't treason punishable by death?

Had she used him to facilitate her escape? Had she? Had this been a trap into which he had all-too-willingly fallen?

'How many men have you had?' he demanded suddenly.

She stared at him in disbelief. 'Have you heard a

word I've just been saying? How many women have *you* had?'

'That's irrelevant!' he snapped. 'So I shall ask you again, Sara—and this time I want an answer. How many?'

'Oh, hundreds,' she retorted, but the expression on his face made her backtrack and even though she despised herself for wanting to salvage her reputation—it didn't stop her from doing it. 'If you must know—I've had one experience before you. One—and it was awful. An ill-judged foray into the sexual arena with a man I'd convinced myself could mean something to me, but I was wrong.' Just as she'd been wrong about so many things at the time.

'Who was he?'

'You think I'm crazy enough to tell you his name?' She shook her head, not wanting to reveal any more than she had to. She didn't want Suleiman to know that at the time she'd been on a mission—trying to convince herself that there were men other than him. That she'd wanted another man to make her feel the way he did. But she had been hoping in vain because no man had even come close. He affected her in a way she had no control over. Even now, with this terrible atmosphere which had descended upon them, he was still making her *feel* stuff, wasn't he? He still made her feel totally *alive* whenever she was near him.

'I was experimenting,' she said. 'Trying to experience the same things as other women my age, but it didn't work.'

'So you conveniently forgot about your planned marriage?'

'You didn't seem to have much difficulty forgetting it, did you? And surely that's the most glaring hypocrisy of all. It wasn't just me who broke the rules. It took two of us to make love just now, and you were one very willing partner. I'm wondering how that registers on your particular scale of loyalty?'

Something in the atmosphere shifted and changed and his face tightened as he nodded.

'You are right, of course. Thank you for reminding me that my own behaviour certainly doesn't give me the right to censure yours. But before we go, just answer me one thing. Did you set out to seduce me, knowing that having sex with me would put an end to your betrothal?'

She hesitated, but only for a moment. 'No,' she said and then, because it felt like a heavy burden, she told him the truth. 'I planned to do something like that, but in the end I couldn't go through with it.'

'Why not?'

She shrugged and suddenly the threat of tears seemed very real as she thought of the boy who had been sold by his mother. 'Because of what you told me about how you and Murat met. How he'd saved your life and how close you'd been when you were growing up. I realised what a big deal your friendship was and how much it meant to you. That's why I ran away.'

'Only I came after you,' he said slowly. 'And seduced you anyway.'

'Yes.' She kept swallowing—the way they told you

to do in aircraft, to stop your ears from popping. But this was to stop the welling tears from falling down over her face. Because tears wouldn't help anyone, would they? They made a woman look weak and a man take control. And she wasn't going to be that woman. 'Yes, you did.'

'I appreciate your honesty,' he said. 'And at least you've concentrated my mind on what needs to happen next.'

She heard the finality in his tone and guessed what was coming next. 'You mean you'll take me to the airfield?'

'So that you can run away again? I don't think so. Isn't it time that you stopped running and faced up to the consequences of your actions? Maybe it's time we both did.' He gave a grim smile and stood up, magnificent and unashamed in his nakedness. 'My brief was to deliver you to the Sultan and that's exactly what I'm going to do.'

She stared at him in bewilderment and then in fear as his body blocked out the fierce light of the sun. All she could see was the powerful shape of his silhouette and suddenly he seemed more than a little intimidating. 'You're still planning to take me to the Sultan?'

'I am.'

'You can't do that.'

'Just watch me.'

She licked her lips. 'He'll kill me.'

'He'll have to kill me first. Don't be absurd, Sara.' He flicked her a glance. 'And don't move. At least, not yet.'

She didn't know what he meant until he walked over to his horse and took a bottle from his saddle-bag, dousing his headdress with a generous slug of water before coming back to her. His face was grave as he crouched down to wipe her belly clean and Sara felt her cheeks flame, because the peculiar intimacy of having Suleiman removing his dried seed from her skin was curiously poignant.

'Removing all traces of yourself?' she questioned.

'You think it's that easy? I wish.' His bitter tone matched hers and she could see the angry gleam of his eyes. 'Now get dressed, Sara—and we will ride together to the palace.'

CHAPTER SEVEN

THE SUN WAS low in the sky when Sara and Suleiman brought their horses to a dusty halt outside the gates of the Sultan's summer residence. Before them, the vast palace towered majestically—its golden hues reflecting the endless desert sands which surrounded it. It was the first time Sara had ever seen the fabled building, and on any other occasion she might have taken time to admire the magnificent architecture with all its soaring turrets and domes. But today her heart was full of dread as she thought of what lay ahead.

What on earth was she going to say to the man she had now spurned in the most dramatic way possible? She had never loved the Sultan, nor wanted him—but never in a million years had she wanted it to turn out this way. She didn't want to hurt him, or—which was much more likely—hurt his pride.

Would he want to punish her? Punish her brother and his kingdom?

The reality began to soak into her skin, which was still glowing after her passionate encounter with the man who had ridden by her side. No matter what happened next—she wasn't going to regret what had just taken place. It might have been wrong, but the words she had whispered to Suleiman just before he had thrust into her had been true. It had felt so right.

She shot a glance at him as he brought his horse to a halt but his stony profile gave nothing away and she suspected that his body language was deliberately forbidding. He hadn't spoken a word to her since that uncomfortable showdown after they'd made love. He had kept busy with the practicalities of preparing to return. And then he had turned on her and hissed that she was nothing but a temptation, silencing her protests with an angry wave of his hand before phoning ahead to let the Sultan's staff know that they were on their way.

Sara looked up at the wide blue bowl of the desert sky as another band of fear gripped her. If ever she had thought she'd felt trapped before—she was quickly discovering a whole new meaning to the word. Here was one hostile man taking her to confront another—and she had no idea of what the outcome would be.

Her instinct was to turn and head in the opposite direction—but during the ride she had thought about what Suleiman had said.

You've spent your whole life running away?

Had she? It was weird seeing yourself through somebody else's eyes. She'd always thought that she was an intrepid sort of person. That she had shown true backbone by setting up on her own in London, far away from her pampered life. It was disturbing to think that maybe there was a kernel of truth in Suleiman's accusation.

Their approach had obviously been observed from

within the palace complex, for the tall gates silently opened and they walked their horses through onto the gravelled forecourt. Sara became aware of the massed blooms of white flowers and their powerful scent which pervaded the air. A white-robed servant came towards them, briefly bowing to her before turning to Suleiman and speaking to him in Qurhahian.

'The Sultan wishes to extend his warmest greeting, Suleiman Abd al-Aziz. He has instructed me to tell you that your chambers are fully prepared—and that you will both rest and recuperate before joining him for dinner later.'

'No.'

Suleiman's denial rang out so emphatically that Sara was startled, for she knew that the language of the desert was couched in much more formal—sometimes flowery—tones. She saw the look of surprise on the servant's face.

'The princess may wish to avail herself of the Sultan's hospitality,' said Suleiman. 'But it is imperative that I speak to His Imperial Majesty without further delay. Please take me to him now.'

Sara could see the servant's confusion but such was the force of Suleiman's personality that the man merely nodded in bewildered consent. He led them through the huge carved doors, speaking rapidly into an incongruously modern walkie-talkie handset which he pulled from his white robes.

Once inside, where several female servants had gathered together in a small group, Suleiman turned to her, his features shadowed and unreadable. 'You will go with these women and they will bathe you,' he instructed.

'But—'

'No buts, Sara. I mean it. This is my territory, not yours. Let me deal with it.'

Sara opened her mouth, then shut it again as she felt a wave of relief wash over her. Was it cowardly of her to want to lean on Suleiman and him to take over? 'Thank you,' she said.

'For what?' he questioned in English, his sudden switch of language seeming to emphasise the bitterness of his tone. 'For taking what was never mine to take? Just go. *Go.*'

He stood perfectly still as she turned away, watching her retreat across the wide, marble entrance hall—his feelings in turmoil; his heart sick with dread. He found himself taking in the unruliness of her hair and the crumpled disorder of her robes. He swallowed. If the Sultan had seen her flushed face, then mightn't he guess the cause of her untidy appearance?

He turned to follow the servant, his heart heavy.

How was he going to be able to tell Murat? How could he possibly admit what had been done? The worst betrayal in the world, from the two people who should have been most loyal to the sovereign.

He was ushered into one of the informal ante-rooms which he recognised from times past. He lifted his gaze to the high, arched ceiling with its intricate mosaic, before the Sultan swept in, alone—his black eyes inscrutable as he subjected his erstwhile emissary to a long, hard look.

'So, Suleiman,' he said. 'This is indeed an unconventional meeting. I was disturbed from playing backgammon at a crucial point in the game, to be told that you wished to see me immediately. Is this true?'

His eyes were questioning and Suleiman felt a terrible wave of sadness wash over him. Once their relationship had been so close that he might have made a joke about his supposed insubordination. And the Sultan would have laughed softly and made a retort in the same vein. But this was no laughing matter.

'Yes, it's true,' he said heavily.

'And may I ask what has provoked this extraordinary break with protocol?'

Suleiman swallowed. 'I have come to tell you that the Princess Sara will not marry you,' he said.

For a moment, the Sultan did not reply. His hawk-like features gave nothing away. 'And should not the princess have told me this herself?' he questioned softly.

Suleiman felt his heart clench as he realised that years of loyalty and friendship now lay threatened by his one stupid act of disloyalty and lust. He had accused Sara of being headstrong—but was not his own behaviour equally reprehensible?

'Sire, I must tell you that I have—'

'No!' The word cracked from Murat's mouth like the sound of a whip and he held up his palm for silence. 'Hold your tongue, Suleiman. If you tell me something I should not hear, then I will have no option than to have you tried for treason.'

'Then so be it!' declared Suleiman, his heart pounding like a piston. 'If that is to be my fate, then I will accept it like a man.'

The Sultan's mouth hardened but he shook his head. 'You think I would do that? You think that a woman— *any woman*—is worth destroying a rare friendship between two men? One which has endured the test of time and all the challenges of hierarchy?'

'I will accept whatever punishment you see fit to bestow on me.'

'You want to slug it out? Is that it?'

Suleiman stared at Murat and, for a moment, the years melted away. Suddenly they were no longer two powerful men with all the burdens and responsibilities which had come with age, but two eight-year-old boys squaring up to each other in the baked dust of the palace stables. It had been soon after Suleiman had been brought from Samahan and he had punched the young Sultan at the height of an argument which had long since been forgotten.

He remembered seeing the shock on Murat's face. The realisation that here was someone who was prepared to take him on. Even to beat him. Murat had waved away the angry courtiers. But he had gone away and taken boxing lessons and, two weeks later, had fought again and soundly beaten Suleiman. After that, the fight victory rate had been spread out evenly.

Suleiman found himself wondering which of them would win, if they fought now. 'No, I don't want to fight you, Sire,' he said. 'But I am concerned about the fall-out, if this scheduled marriage doesn't go ahead.'

'As well you should be concerned!' said Murat

furiously. 'For you know as well as I do that the union was intended as an alliance between the two countries.'

Suleiman nodded. 'Couldn't an alternative solution be offered instead? A new peace agreement drawn up between Qurhah and Dhi'ban—which could finally banish all the years of unrest. After all, a diplomatic solution is surely more modern and appropriate than an old-fashioned dynastic marriage.'

Murat gave a soft laugh. 'Oh, how I miss your skills of diplomacy, Suleiman. As well as your unerring ability to pick out the most beautiful women on our foreign tours.' He gave a reminiscent sigh. 'Some pretty unforgettable women, as I recall.'

But Suleiman's head was too full of concern to be distracted by memories of the sexual shenanigans of the past. 'Is this a feasible plan, do you think, Sire?'

Murat shrugged. 'It's feasible. It's going to take a lot of backroom work and manoeuvring. But it's do-able, yes.'

The two men stared at one another and Suleiman clenched his teeth. 'Now give me my punishment,' he ground out.

There was a brief silence. 'Oh, that's easy. My punishment is for you to take her,' said Murat silkily. 'Take her away with you and do what you will with her. Because I know you—and I know how your mind operates. Countless times I have watched as you grow bored with the inevitable clinginess of the female of the species. She will drive you mad within the month, Suleiman—that much I can guarantee.'

Murat's words were still ringing in Suleiman's ears

as he waited in the sunlit palace courtyard for Sara to emerge from her ablutions. And when she did, with her blonde hair still damp and tightly plaited, he could not prevent the instinctive kick of lust which was quickly followed by the equally potent feeling of regret.

Her face was pale and her eyes dark with anxiety as she looked up at him. 'What did he say?'

'He accepts the situation. The wedding is off.'

'Just like that?'

Suleiman's mouth hardened. What would she say if he told her the truth? That Murat had spoken of her as if she'd been a poisoned chalice he was passing to his former aide. That his punishment was to have her, not to lose her.

He suspected she would never speak to him again. And he wasn't prepared for that to happen.

Not yet.

'He has agreed to make way for a diplomatic solution instead.'

'He has?' Her eyes were filled with confusion as if she found something about his reaction difficult to understand. 'But that's good, isn't it?'

'It is an acceptable compromise, considering the circumstances,' said Suleiman, holding up a jangling set of keys which sparked silver in the bright sunlight. 'Now let's go. We're leaving the horses here and taking one of the Sultan's cars.'

Sara tried to keep up with his long-legged stride as she followed him into the courtyard, but it wasn't until they were sitting in the blessed cool of the air-conditioned car that she could pluck up enough courage to ask him.

'Where are we going?'

He didn't answer straight away. In fact, he didn't answer for a good while. Not until they had left the palace far behind them and all that surrounded them was sand and emptiness. Pulling over onto the side of the wide and deserted road, he unfastened his seat belt before leaning over and undoing hers.

'What...are you doing?' she asked.

'I want to kiss you.'

'Suleiman—'

His mouth was hard and hungry and she could feel his anger coming off him in waves. He slid towards her on the front seat of the luxury car, one hand capturing her breast, while the other began to ruck up the slithery silk of her dress. He stopped kissing her long enough to slide his hand up her bare thigh and stare down at her face.

'Suleiman,' she said again—as if saying his name would make some kind of sense of the situation. As if it would remind her that this was dangerous—in so many ways.

'All I can think of is you,' he said. 'All I want is to touch you again. You're driving me crazy.'

She swallowed as he edged his fingertip inside her panties. 'This isn't the answer.'

'Isn't it?'

He had reached her core now, touching her exquisitely aroused flesh so that the scent of her sex overrode the subtle perfume of the rose petals in which she'd bathed.

'No. It's…oh, Suleiman. That's not fair.'

'Who said anything about fairness?'

His finger brushed against the sensitive nub. 'Oh,' she breathed. And again. *'Oh.'*

'Still think this isn't the answer?'

She shook her head and Suleiman felt an undeniable burst of triumph as she fell back against the leather seat and spread her legs for him. But his mouth was grim as he rubbed his finger against her sex and all kinds of dark emotions stirred within him.

He distracted himself by watching her writhe with pleasure. He watched the flush of colour which spread over her skin like wildfire and felt the change in her body as her back began to arch. Her little cries became louder. Her legs stiffened as they stretched out in front of her and he saw a flash of something—was it anger or regret?—before her eyelids fluttered to a close and she cried out his name, even though he got the idea she was trying very hard not to.

Afterwards she smoothed down her tunic with trembling fingers and turned to him and there was a look on her face he'd never seen before. She looked satiated yes, but determined too—her eyes flashing violet fire as she lifted up his robes.

'Now what are you doing?' he questioned.

'You ask too many questions.'

She freed an erection which was so hard that it hurt—and sucked him until he came in her mouth almost immediately. And he had never felt so powerless in his life. Nor so turned on. Afterwards, he opened his eyes to look at her but she was staring straight ahead, her shoulders stiff with tension and her jaw set.

'Sara?' he questioned.

She turned her head and he was shocked by the pallor of her face, which made her eyes look like two glittering violet jewels. 'What?'

He picked up one of her hands, which was lying limply in her lap, and raised it to his lips and kissed it. 'You didn't enjoy that?'

She shrugged. 'On one level, yes, of course I did—as, I imagine, did you. But that wasn't about sex, was it, Suleiman? That seemed to be more about anger than anything else. I think I can understand why you're feeling it, but I don't particularly like it.'

'You were angry too,' he said softly.

She turned her head to look at the endless stretch of sand outside the window. 'I was feeling things other than anger,' she said.

'What things?'

'Oh, you know. Stupid things. Regret. Sadness. The realisation that nothing ever stays the same.' She turned back to him, telling herself to be strong. Telling herself that the friendship they'd shared so long ago had been broken by time and circumstance. And now by desire. And that made her want to bury her face in her hands and weep.

She forced a smile. 'So now we're done—are you going to take me to the airfield so I can go back to England?'

He reached his hand out to touch her face, sliding

his thumb against her parted lips so that they trembled. Leaning over, he hovered his lips over hers. '*Are we done?*'

Briefly, Sara closed her eyes. *Say yes,* she told herself. *It's the only sane solution. You've escaped the marriage and you know there's no future in this.* Her lashes fluttered open to stare straight into the obsidian gleam of his eyes. His mouth was still close enough for her to feel the warmth of his breath and she struggled against the temptation to kiss him.

Were they done?

In her heart, she thought they were.

She ought to go back to England and start again. She should go back to her job at Gabe's—if he would have her—and carry on as before. As if nothing had happened.

She bit her lip, because it wasn't that easy. Because something *had* happened and how could she go back to the way she'd been before? She felt different now because she *was* different. Inevitably. She had been freed from a marriage in which she'd had no say, but she was confused. Her future looked just as bewildering as before and it was all because of Suleiman.

She had tried burying memories of him, but that hadn't worked. And now that she'd made love with him, it had stirred up all the feelings she had repressed for so long. It had stirred up a sexual hunger which was eating away at her even now—minutes after he'd just brought her to orgasm in the front seat of the Sultan's car. It didn't matter what she *thought* she should do—

because, when push came to shove, she was putty in his hands. When Suleiman touched her, he set her on fire.

And maybe that was the answer. Maybe she just needed time to convince herself that his arrogance would be intolerable in the long term. If she tore herself away from him now—before she'd had her fill of him—wouldn't she be caught in the same old cycle of forever wanting him?

'Do you have a better suggestion?' she questioned.

'I do. A much better one.' He stroked his hand down over her plaited hair. 'We could take my plane and fly off somewhere.'

'Where?'

'Anywhere you like. As long as there's a degree of comfort. I'm done with desert sand and making out in the front seat, like a couple of teenagers. I want to take you to bed and stay there for a week.'

CHAPTER EIGHT

'SO WHY PARIS?' Sara questioned, her mouth full of croissant.

Suleiman leaned across the rumpled sheets and used the tip of his finger to rescue a stray fragment of pastry which had fallen onto her bare breast. He lifted the finger to his mouth and sucked on it, his dark eyes not leaving her face.

And Sara wanted to kiss him all over again. She wanted to fling her arms around him and press her body against him and close her eyes and have him colour her world wonderful. Because that was what it was like whenever he touched her.

'It's my favourite hotel,' he said. 'And there is a reason why it's known as the city of lovers. We can lie in bed all day and nobody bats an eyelid. We need never set foot outside the door if we don't want to.'

'Well, that's convenient,' said Sara drily. 'Because that's exactly what we've being doing. We've hardly seen any of the sights. In fact, we've been here for three days and I haven't even been up the Eiffel Tower.'

He kissed her nipple. 'And do you want to go up the Eiffel Tower?'

'Maybe.' Sara put her plate down and leant back against the snowy bank of pillows. That thing he was doing to her nipple with his tongue was distracting her from her indolent breakfast in bed, but there were other things on her mind. Questions which kept flitting into her mind and which, no matter how hard she tried, wouldn't seem to flit away again. She had told herself that there was a good reason why you were supposed to live in the present—but sometimes you just couldn't prevent thoughts of the future from starting to darken the edges of your mind. Or the past, come to that...

She kept her voice light and airy. As if she were asking him nothing more uncomplicated than would he please order her a coffee from room service. 'Have you brought other women here?'

There was a pause. The fingers which had been playing with her nipple stilled against the puckered flesh. He slanted her a look which she found more rueful than reassuring. 'What do you want me to say? That you're the first?'

'No, of course not,' she said stiffly. 'I didn't imagine for a moment that I was.'

But the thought of other women lying where she was lying unsettled her more than it should have done. Actually, it didn't unsettle her—it hurt. The thought of Suleiman licking someone *else's* breasts made dark and hateful thoughts crowd into her head. The image of him sliding his tongue between another woman's legs made her feel almost dizzy with rage. And jealousy. And a million other things she had no right to feel.

She should have known this would happen. She should have listened to all the doubts she'd refused to listen to that day in the desert. When she'd been so hungry for him and so impressed—yes, impressed—when he'd offered to fly her anywhere in the world that she'd smiled the smile of a besotted woman and said yes.

And now look what had happened. Her feelings for him hadn't died, that was for sure. She still cared for him—more than she wanted to care for him and more than it was safe to care. Yet deep down she knew that this trip was supposed to be about getting the whole *passion* thing out of their system. For both of them. Something which had begun so messily needed to have a clean ending so that they could both move on; she knew that, too.

So what had happened?

Suleiman had pulled out all the stops—that was what had happened. He was a man she had always adored, and now he had an added wow factor, because his vast self-made wealth gave him an undeniable glamour. And glamour mixed with desire made for a very powerful cocktail indeed.

He had whisked her onto his own, private jet—and she'd got the distinct feeling that he had enjoyed showing it off—and flown her to a city she'd never got around to visiting before. That was the first mistake. Was it a good idea to go to the city of romance if you were trying to convince yourself that you weren't still in love with a man?

He had booked them into the presidential suite at the Georges V, where the staff all seemed to know him by name. Sara had been brought up in a palace, so she knew pretty much everything there was to know about luxury, but she fell in love with the iconic Parisian hotel.

Next he took her shopping. Not just, as he said, because she had brought only a very inappropriate wardrobe with her—but because he wanted to buy her things. She told him that she would prefer to buy things for herself. He told her that simply wasn't acceptable. There was a short stand-off, followed by a making-up session which had involved a bowl of whipped cream and a lot of imagination. And because she felt weak from all their love-making and dizzy just with the sense of *being* there—she went ahead and let him buy her the stuff anyway.

The crisp January weather was cold so he splashed out on an ankle-length sheepskin coat and some thigh-high leather boots.

'But you disapproved when I was wearing a very similar pair back in England,' she had objected.

'Yes, but these are for my eyes only,' he'd purred, pillowing his head against his folded arms as he'd leaned back against the sofa to watch her slide them on when they had arrived back at the hotel with their purchases. 'And they will look very good when worn with nothing but a pair of panties.'

Ah, yes. Panties. That seemed to be another area of his expertise. He indulged her taste for lingerie with tiny, wispy bras designed to highlight her nipples. He bought her an outrageous pair of crotchless panties and later on that day proved just what a time-effective purchase they could be. Silky camiknickers and matching suspender belts were added to the costly pile he accumulated in the city's most exclusive store, with Suleiman displaying an uncanny knack of knowing just what would suit her.

Sara sat up in bed and brushed away the last few crumbs of croissant. 'How many?' she questioned, getting out of bed and feeling acutely aware that he was watching her.

He frowned. 'How many what?'

'Women.' She walked across the room towards the windows, wondering why she had gone ahead and asked him a question she had vowed not to ask.

'Sara,' he said softly. 'It's knowing women as I do which allows me to give you so much pleasure.'

'Yes,' she said, staring fixedly out of the giant windows which commanded a stunning view of the city, where the Eiffel Tower dominated a landscape made light by the shimmering waters of the Seine. 'I imagine it is.'

She listened to the sudden sound of silence which had descended on the room. One of those silences between two people which she'd realised could say so much. Or rather, so little. Silences when she had to fight to bite back the words which were bursting to come out. Words which had been building up inside her for days—years—and which she knew he wouldn't want to hear.

Instead, she stared out at the cityscape in front of

her as if it was the most wonderful thing she'd ever seen, which wasn't easy when her vision was starting to get all blurred.

'Sara?'

She shook her head, praying that he wouldn't pursue it. *Leave me alone. Let me get over it in my own time.*

'Sara, look at me.'

It took a moment or two before she had composed herself enough to turn around and curve him a bright smile. 'What?'

His eyes were narrowed and speculative. 'Are those *tear*s I see?'

'No, of course it isn't,' she said, dabbing furiously at her eyes with a bunched fist. 'And if it is, then it's only my damned hormones. You must know all about those.'

'Come here.'

'I don't want to. I'm enjoying the view.'

His gaze slid over her naked body. 'I'm enjoying the view too, but I want you to come back to bed and tell me what's wrong.'

She considered refusing—but what else was she going to do in this vast arena of the bedroom, with Suleiman watching her like that? She felt vulnerable—and not just because she was naked. She felt vulnerable with each hour of every day, knowing she was losing her heart to him.

He held out his arms and she felt as if she'd lost some kind of battle as she went to him, loving the way the flat of his hand smoothed down the spill of her hair as she climbed into bed beside him. She loved the feel of his naked body entwined with hers. She snuggled up to him, hoping that her closeness would distract him enough to stop asking questions she had no desire to answer. But no. He tilted up her chin, so that there was nowhere to look except into the ebony gleam of his eyes.

'Want to talk about it, princess?'

She shook her head. 'Not really.'

'Shall I guess?'

'Please don't, Suleiman. It's not important.'

'I think it is. You're falling in love with me.'

Sara flinched. Maybe she wasn't as good at hiding her feelings as she'd thought. But then, neither was Suleiman as clever as *he* thought. He'd got the sentiment right—but the tense was wrong. She wasn't 'falling' in love with him—she'd *always* been in love with him. Fancy him not knowing that. She gave him a cool smile. 'That's an occupational hazard for you, I expect?'

'Yes,' he said seriously. 'I'm afraid it is.'

She shook her head, laughing in spite of everything. 'You really are the most arrogant man I've ever known.'

'I have never denied my arrogance.'

'Admitting that doesn't make it all right!'

She was trying to wriggle out of his arms, but he was having none of it. He captured both her wrists in his hands, stilling her so that their eyes were on a collision course.

'I can't help who I am, Sara. And I have enough experience—'

'And then some.'

'To recognise when a woman starts to lose her heart

to me. Sweetheart, will you please stop wriggling—and glaring—and listen to what I have to say?'

'I don't want to listen.'

'I think you need to.'

She stilled in his arms, aware of the loud thunder of her heart. His hard thigh was levered between her own and a sadness suddenly swept over her—because wasn't she going to miss being in bed with him like this? Cuddled up in his arms and feeling as if the rest of the world didn't exist. 'I don't want to turn this into a long goodbye,' she whispered.

'And neither do I.' He tucked a strand of hair behind her ear and sighed. 'I thought I did.'

'What do you mean, you thought you did?'

Suleiman stared at her, as if unsure how much to tell her. But this was Sara—and hadn't his relationship with her always been special and unique? The usual rules didn't apply to this blonde-haired beauty he'd known since she was a mixed-up little kid. 'Usually when a woman reaches this stage, I begin to grow wary. Bored.'

'This *stage*?' she spluttered indignantly. 'You mean, as if this is some kind of infectious disease you're incubating!'

He laughed. 'I know that sounds like more arrogance but I'm trying to tell you the truth,' he said. 'Or would you rather me dress it up with lavish compliments and make like you're the only woman I've ever been intimate with?'

'No,' she said, unable to keep the slight sulk from her voice.

'At this stage of an affair,' he said, though his mocking smile didn't lessen the impact of his words, 'I usually recognise that it must come to an end, no matter how much desire I'm feeling. Because an inequality of affection can prove volatile—and I have never wished to play games of emotional cruelty.'

'Good of you,' she said sarcastically. Her heart was beating painfully against her ribcage as she waited to hear what was coming next. But she kept her face as impassive as possible because she wasn't going to give him the chance to reject her. Not a second time. And if that made it seem as if all she cared about was her pride—so what? What else was she going to be left with in the long, lonely hours when he'd gone?

She forced a smile, hoping that she seemed all grown up and reasonable. Because she was not going to be the woman with the red eyes, clinging to his legs as he walked out of the door. 'Look, Suleiman—you've been very honest with me, so let me return the compliment. I've always had a crush on you—ever since I was a young girl. We both know that. That's one of the reasons that kiss when I was eighteen turned into so much more.'

'That kiss changed my life,' he said simply.

Sara felt the clamp of pain around her heart. *Don't tell me things like that, because I'll read into them more than you want me to.* 'This time in Paris has been...great. You know it has. You're the most amazing lover. I'm sure I'm not the first woman to have told you that.' She sucked in a deep breath, because she was sure she wouldn't be the last, either. 'But we both know this isn't going anywhere—and we mustn't make it into more than it is, because that will spoil it. We both know that when something is put out of reach, it makes that something seem much more tantalising. That's why—'

He silenced her by placing his finger over her lips and his black eyes burned into hers. 'I think I love you.'

Sara froze. Wasn't it funny how you could dream of a man saying those words to you? And then he did and it was nothing like how you thought it would be. For a start, he had qualified them. He *thought* he loved her? That was the kind of thing someone said when they took an umbrella out on a sunny day. *I thought it might rain.* She didn't believe him. She didn't dare believe him.

'Don't say that,' she hissed.

He looked startled. 'Even if it's true?'

'Especially if it's true,' she said, and burst into tears.

Perplexed, Suleiman stared at her and tightened his arms around her waist as he felt her tears dripping down his neck. 'What have I done wrong?'

'Nothing!'

'Then why are you crying?'

She shook her head, her words coming out between gulps of swallowed air. Words he could hardly make out but which included 'always', quickly contradicted by 'never' and then, when she'd managed to snatch enough breath back, finishing rather inexplicably with 'hopeless'.

Eventually, she raised a tear-stained face to his. 'Don't you understand, you stupid man?' she whispered. 'I think I love you too.'

'Then why are you crying like that?'

'Because it can never work!' she said fiercely. 'How could it?'

'Why not?'

'Because our lives are totally incompatible, that's why.' She rubbed her hand over her wet cheek. 'You live in Samahan and I live in London. You are an oil baron and I'm a flaky artist.'

'You think those things are insurmountable?' he demanded. 'You don't imagine these are the kind of logistical problems which other couples might have overcome?'

Sara shook her head as all her old fears came crowding back. She thought of her own mother. Love certainly hadn't brought *her* happiness, had it? Because love was just a feeling. A feeling which had no guarantee of lasting. She and Suleiman had both experienced something when they were fixed at a time and in a place which was light years away from their normal lives. How could something like that possibly survive if it was transplanted into the separate worlds which they both inhabited?

'Listen to me, Suleiman,' she said. 'We don't really *know* one another.'

'That's completely untrue. I have known you since you were seven years old. I certainly know you better than I know any other woman.'

'Not as adults. Not properly. We have no idea if we're compatible.'

His hand tightened around her waist; his thumb

traced a provocative little circle. 'I think we're *ve-ry* compatible.'

'That's not the kind of compatibility I was talking about.'

'No?'

'No. I'm not talking about snatched moments of forbidden passion beneath the shade of a rock in the desert. Or sex-filled weekends at one of the best hotels in the world. I'm talking about normal life, Suleiman. Everyday life. The kind of life we all have to lead— whether we're a princess or an oil magnate, or the man who drives the grocery truck.' She pulled away from him so she could look at him properly. 'Tell me what your dream scenario would be. Where you'd like us to go from here—if you had the choice.'

'Well, that bit's easy.' He tugged at the end of a long strand of hair which was tickling his chest. 'You no longer have a job, do you?'

'Not officially, no. I left Gabe a letter on Christmas Eve, saying I'd had to go away suddenly and I wasn't sure when I was coming back. It's not the kind of thing his employees usually do and I'm not sure if he'd ever employ me again. There's a long list of people desperate to fill my shoes. He's the best in the business who could get anyone to work for him. I doubt whether he'd give another chance to someone who could let him down without any warning.'

But if she was hoping to see some sort of remorse on Suleiman's face, she was in for a disappointment. The slow smile which curved his lips made the little hairs on the back of her neck stand up, because she suspected she wasn't going to like what she heard next.

'Perfect,' he said.

'I fail to see what's perfect about leaving my boss in the lurch and not having any kind of secure future to go back to.'

'But that's the point, Sara. You do have a secure future—just a different kind of future from the one you envisaged.' He smiled at her as if he had just discovered that all his shares had risen by ten per cent while they'd been in bed. 'You don't have to go back to working for a large organisation. All that—what do they say?—clocking in and clocking out. Buying your lunch in a paper bag and eating it at your desk.'

'Gabe happens to run a very large staff canteen,' she said coldly. 'And insists on all his staff taking a proper lunch break. And I think it's you who are missing the point. I *want* to go back to work. It's what I do. What else do you suggest I do?'

He tugged on another strand of blonde hair and began to wind it around his finger. 'Simple. You come back to Samahan, with me.'

She stared at him in disbelief. 'Samahan?'

His eyes narrowed. 'The expression on your face looks as if I have suggested that you make your home in Hades. But I think you will find yourself greatly surprised. Samahan has improved greatly since the cross-border wars. The discovery of oil has brought with it much wealth and we are ploughing some of that wealth back into the land.'

He let go of the twisted strand of hair and it dangled in front of her bare breast, in a perfect blonde ringlet.

'My home will not disappoint you, Sara—for it is as vast as any palace and just as beautiful. A world-class architect from Uruguay designed it for me, and I flew in a rose expert from the west coast of America to design my gardens. I stable my horses there—two of them won medals in the last Olympics. I have a great team around me.'

Sara recognised what he was doing. This was the modern equivalent of a male gorilla beating his chest. He was showing her how much he had achieved against the odds—he, the poor boy whose own mother had sold him. He was trying to reassure her that he would treat her like a princess, but that was just what she didn't want. She had hated her life as a princess, which was why she had left it far behind.

'And what would I do all day in this beautiful house of yours?'

'You would make love to me.'

'Obviously that's extremely tempting.' Her smile didn't slip. 'But how about when you're not around? When you're jetting off to the States or swanning off somewhere being an oil baron?'

'You can amuse yourself, for there is much that you will enjoy. Swim in the pool. Explore my extensive library.'

'Just like one long holiday, you mean?' she questioned brightly.

'Not necessarily. You will find a role for yourself there, Sara. I know you will. I think you will find that the desert lands are changing. How long is it since you visited the region?'

'Years,' she said distractedly. 'And I think you'd better stop right there. It's very sweet of you and I'm sure your home is perfectly lovely, but I don't want to go to Samahan. I want to go back to London because there are still loose ends to tie up. I owe Gabe an explanation about what happened and I want to finish up the project I was working on.' Her eyes met his. She realised that she wanted him and loved him enough to want to try to make it work. So why not reverse his question to her? 'But you could come back with me, if you like.'

'With you?' His black eyes were hooded.

'Why not? We can see if we can exist compatibly there—and if we can, then I'll think about giving Samahan a try. Does that sound reasonable?'

She saw the sudden hardening of his lips and realised that 'reasonable' was not on the top of Suleiman's agenda. He wasn't used to having his wishes thwarted, particularly not by a woman. He had expected her to fall in with his plans—without stopping to think that she might have plans of her own.

But was he seriously suggesting she might be happy being ensconced in what sounded like the luxury prison of his desert home? Hadn't that been what she'd spent her whole life rebelling against?

'What do you think?' she questioned tentatively.

He slipped his hand between her legs. 'I think we have wasted enough time talking about geographical escape.'

'Suleiman—'

He bent his head to her neck and kissed it.

'You want me to stop?'

'That's the last thing I want.'

She thought she heard soft triumph in his laugh as he sheathed himself in a condom and then lay back against the mattress with a look of satisfaction on his face. *Like a conquering hero,* she thought as he lifted her up like a trophy, hating the part of her which enjoyed that.

His moan echoed hers as he slid her down slowly onto his erection. With each angled thrust of her hips she took him deeper and deeper and she wondered what he was thinking. She knew he was watching her as her blonde hair swung wild and free—and suddenly she found herself *performing* for him.

Was she trying to prove that she was a match for all those women who had preceded her—by playing with her breasts and biting her lips, her eyes closed as if she was indulging in some wild and secret fantasy?

Whatever it was, it seemed to work because he went crazy for her. Crazier than she'd ever known him. He splayed his dark hands possessively over her hips as he made the penetration deeper still. And each time she was close to orgasm, he stopped. Stopped so that once she actually screamed out loud with pent-up frustration, because he made her build it up all over again.

He did it to her over and over again. Until she begged him to release her and then at last he slid her onto the floor and drove into her, as if it were the very first time all over again. She felt her body shatter with the most powerful orgasm she'd ever known but once it began to recede, she felt a sudden sense of unease.

An unease which grew stronger with every second. Because that had been all about power, hadn't it? Suleiman was a man who was used to getting his own way and by refusing to conform to his wishes she had taken control of the situation. She had taken control and he would use whatever it took to get it back.

Sex.

Power.

Palaces.

Even words of love which sounded wonderful, until you wondered if he actually knew what they meant. Were they just another lever to get her to see things his way? she wondered.

He'd never even seen her in her usual environment. He didn't *know* that very important side of her personality.

'I want to go back to London,' she said stubbornly. 'Do you want to come with me or not?'

CHAPTER NINE

'SAY THAT AGAIN.'

Bathed in the light which flooded into Gabe Steel's enormous penthouse office, Sara met her boss's eyes as he drawled his question. He was leaning back in his chair with a look of curiosity in his grey eyes. And Gabe didn't usually do curiosity. At least, not with his employees. She guessed that leaving him a rather dramatic letter saying she was going away and then asking to be reinstated just a few weeks later was enough to stir anyone's interest. Even your incredibly high-powered and often cynical boss.

'I know it sounds incredible,' she said.

He laughed. 'Incredible is something of an understatement, Sara. How come you kept it a secret for so long?'

She shrugged. 'Oh, you know. I'd hate to make out that I'm some poor little rich girl—but everyone treats you differently once they know you're a princess.'

'I guess they do.' His pewter eyes narrowed as he twirled a solid gold pen between his long fingers. 'So what's brought about the sudden change of heart?'

Change of heart.

She wondered if Gabe had any idea of how un-cannily accurate that particular phrase was. Prob-ably. You didn't get to be head of one of the world's biggest advertising agencies without having a finely tuned degree of insight.

'I was…' She wondered what he would say if she told him the truth. *I was due to get married to a Sultan, but I put a stop to that particular arrangement by having sex with his closest friend.* Probably not a good idea. Men could be notoriously tribal about that kind of thing and she didn't want to portray Suleiman as some sort of bad guy. And anyway, that wasn't the whole truth, was it? Suleiman wasn't the *reason* be-hind the cancelled wedding. He was just a symptom.

She stared sightlessly out of the penthouse window. A symptom who was currently prowling around her London apartment and making her feel as if she had imprisoned a tiger there.

It was a big apartment—everyone said so. So how come the rooms seemed to have shrunk to the size of matchboxes since Suleiman had accompanied her back from Paris and moved in with her? It had been her mother's apartment and Sara loved every inch of it, a feeling clearly not shared by her lover.

He had walked through the three huge—or so she'd thought—reception rooms, had barely deigned to look at the kitchen and had given the bedrooms only a cursory glance, before turning to demand where the garden was.

She had hated the way her voice had sounded all defensive. 'There isn't one.'

'No garden?' He had sounded incredulous, while all her explanations about the convenience of having a nearby park had fallen on deaf ears.

He had complained about the plumbing—which admittedly *was* fairly ancient—and insisted on having black-out blinds installed in her bedroom. He had commandeered the second bedroom as some kind of makeshift office. Suddenly emails began arriving at odd times of the day and night. Important documents from the US and the Middle East were delivered daily, while a series of efficient sounding staff would ring and she would hear him speaking in his native tongue. She told him it was like living at the United Nations.

He said he was trying to decide whether or not to set up a London headquarters. But that was a big decision which couldn't be made in a hurry, while Sara seemed to get stuck with the smaller, niggling ones.

She'd been forced to find some kind of laundry service since it seemed that Suleiman liked to change his shirt at least twice a day. It helped explain why he always looked so immaculate, but the practicalities of such high sartorial standards were a pain.

But she tried to tell herself that these were just glitches which could easily be sorted out. That Suleiman had never lived with anyone before and neither had she. She convinced herself that all these problems were solvable, but quickly realised there was one which wasn't—and that was the problem of time management. Or rather, *her* time management. Suleiman was obviously used to having women at his beck and call. He didn't like it when she got up at seven each morning to get ready for work. Sometimes it seemed as if he was almost *jealous* of her job.

And that scared her.

It scared her even more than her growing feelings for him.

It was as if the love she felt for Suleiman had started out as a tiny seed, which was in danger of becoming a rampant plant and spreading its tentacles everywhere. His presence was so pervasive and his character so compelling that she felt as if she was being taken over by him. That if she allowed him to, he would take over her whole life and completely dominate her and she would become invisible. And she couldn't allow him to do that.

She didn't dare do that.

So even though she had to fight every loving and lustful instinct in her body, she didn't give in to Suleiman's repeated attempts to push her job into second place.

'Come back to bed,' he would purr, with that tiger-hasn't-been-fed look on his face, as he patted the empty space on the bed beside him.

And Sara would pull on her silk wrap and move to a safe distance away from him. 'I can't do that or I'll be late,' she'd said primly, the third time it happened. 'Haven't you ever been out with a working woman before—and if so, how on earth did you cope?'

His answering smile had been infuriating. Almost, she thought—*smug.*

'Most women can be persuaded to take a sabbatical, if you make it worth their while.'

Sara had felt sick at the lengths to which her sex would go in order to hang onto a man. Which, of course, made her even more determined not to weaken. Her job meant independence and she'd fought long and hard for it.

She realised that Gabe was still looking at her from the other side of the desk. Still waiting for some kind of explanation. She flashed him a slightly self-conscious smile.

'Actually, it's a man.'

'It usually is,' he offered drily. 'Would that be the reason why you had your skirt on inside out yesterday morning?'

'Oh, Gabe!' She clapped her palms to her flaming cheeks. 'I'm so sorry. I only realised when I came out of the meeting and Alice pointed it out.'

'Forget it. I only mention it because the client did—so perhaps best not to repeat it. Anyway.' He smiled. 'What's his name? This man.'

She could hear her voice softening as she said it. 'It's Suleiman Abd al-Aziz—'

Gabe's eyes narrowed 'The oil baron?'

'You've heard of him?'

He smiled. 'Unlike princesses, global magnates tend not to stay anonymous for very long.'

'No, I suppose not. The thing is, I was thinking…' She twisted her fingers together in her lap and wondered what was making her feel so nervous. Actually, that wasn't true. She knew exactly what was making her nervous. On some instinctive level, she was terrified of Suleiman meeting her powerful and very sexy boss. 'I wanted Suleiman to get a bit of an idea about what my job's about. I told him about the massive campaign we did for that new art gallery in Whitechapel—and I thought that I might bring him along to the opening tonight. If that's all right.'

'Excellent. You do that.' Gabe looked at her expectantly. 'And now, if we're through with all the personal details—can you get me the drawings for the Hudson account?'

Noting the slight reprimand, Sara opened up the folder she'd carried in with her and worked hard on the account for the rest of the afternoon. She sent Alice out for coffee and tried ringing Suleiman to tell him about the gallery opening, but he wasn't answering his phone.

It was gone six by the time she arrived back home to find the apartment filled with the smell of cinnamon and oranges. She wondered if Suleiman had ordered something in and whether he'd just forgotten that she had the opening tonight.

Because mealtimes had proved another stumbling block, mainly because Suleiman was used to having servants cater to his every whim. He liked food to arrive when he wanted it—usually after sex. He was not interested in the mechanics of getting it, not of shopping for it nor having Sara rustle him up a meal. So far they had compromised by eating out every night, but sometimes she just wanted to kick off her shoes and scoff toast on the sofa.

She followed the direction of the aroma out to the

kitchen, and blinked in surprise to see Suleiman leaning over the hob, adding something to a pot. It was
such an incongruous sight—and so rare to see him in
jeans—that for a moment she just stood there, feasting
her eyes on his powerful frame and thick dark hair. The
denim clung to his narrow hips, it hugged the muscu-
lar shaft of his long legs and she had to swallow down
her instant feeling of lust.

'Wow. This is a sight for sore eyes,' she said softly.
'What are you doing?'

'Wondering why it's so difficult to buy fresh apri-
cots in central London.' He turned round, his black
eyes glittering as he curved her a smile. 'Actually, I'm
trying to impress my liberated princess by producing
a meal, after she's spent a hard day at the office.'

Putting her handbag down on the counter, she
walked over to him and looped her arms around his
neck. 'I didn't know you cooked.'

'That's because I rarely do these days. But as you
know, I once served in the Qurhahian army,' he said,
bending to brush his mouth over hers. 'Where even
men who had been spoilt by living in palaces were
taught the basics of food prep.'

She laughed, lifting her lips for a proper kiss and
within seconds she was lost in it. And so was he. Suddenly food was forgotten. Everything was forgotten,
except the need to have him as close to her as possible.
Her fingers tugged at his shirt, pulling it open to reveal
his bare chest—not caring that several buttons went
bouncing all over the stone tiles of the kitchen floor.

She tugged impatiently at his belt and he gave a low

laugh as he pushed her up against the door. Rucking up her dress, he ripped her panties apart and her muffled protest was stifled with a hungry kiss. She could hear the rasp of his zip and the buoyant weight of his erection as it sprang free. She reached down to touch him, her fingertips skating over his silken hardness before he removed her hand. Cushioning the weight of her bottom with his hands, he positioned himself where she was hot and wet for him and thrust deep inside her.

Her legs wrapped tightly around his hips, Sara clung to him as they rocked in rhythm, but it was over very quickly. Her head wilted like a cut flower as she leaned it against his shoulder and her voice was sleepy in his ear.

'Nice,' she murmured.

'Is that the best you can do? I was hoping for something a little more lyrical than "nice".'

'Would stupendous work better?'

'Stupendous is a good word,' he said.

'Listen.' She kissed his neck. 'Do you want to go to the opening of that gallery in Whitechapel? The one I told you about? It's tonight.'

He lifted up a handful of hair and brushed his lips against her neck. 'No, I don't—and neither do you. Let's just stay home. I'm making dinner and afterwards I'm sure we can find ways to amuse ourselves.'

Sara could feel the warmth of her orgasm beginning to ebb away. 'Suleiman, I have to go.'

'No, you don't. You don't *have* to go anywhere. You've been working all day as it is.'

'I know I have. But this is my job. Remember?' She

thought of her mother and the way she'd let all her options slide away from her. She thought of the way that men could manoeuvre women into a corner, if you let them. *And she wasn't going to let Suleiman do that to her.* She bent down to pick up the tattered lace which had once been her panties. 'I've been a major part of the whole campaign from the get-go and I want to see the launch. It's expected of me and it would look very odd if I wasn't there. But I asked Gabe whether I could bring you along—and he said yes.'

There was a pause. 'How very generous of him,' he said acidly. 'And you didn't think to give me any notice?'

'Actually, I did.' She tried to ignore the dangerous note in his voice, telling herself that she *had* sprung this on him at the last minute. And why had that been? Because she'd feared just this kind of reaction if she'd said anything about it sooner? 'I tried ringing, but you weren't picking up. Look, you really don't have to go to this, Suleiman, but I do. So I'm going to take a shower and get ready.'

Without another word, she walked into the bedroom and stripped off her clothes before hitting the shower. She half expected Suleiman to follow her, but he didn't.

She was *not* going to feel guilty. Furiously, she lathered shampoo into her hair. If he loved her—as he said he loved her—then shouldn't he be making more of an effort to integrate into her world, and her life?

He could meet Gabe and he'd see Alice again—as well as some of the other graphic designers she'd spoken about. Wasn't that what modern coupledom was all about?

But as she blow-dried her hair in front of the bedroom mirror her fears just wouldn't seem to leave her. She found herself wondering if they were just *playing* at being modern. Pretending that everything was fine, when deep down nothing had really been addressed. At heart, wasn't Suleiman just another old-fashioned desert warrior who was incapable of any real change?

Knowing that the press would be there, as well as the usual smattering of celebrity guests, she was extra generous with the mascara. She could hear the sound of water running in the bathroom next door and moments later Suleiman walked into the bedroom, a towel wrapped around his hips.

He rubbed at his damp hair with a second towel and she thought how powerful his body looked. The whiteness of the towel contrasted against the deep olive of his skin and droplets of water gleamed there, as if he'd been showered with tiny diamonds.

'Oh, good,' she said, and smiled. 'You've decided to come.'

'Reluctantly,' he growled as he pulled a white shirt from the wardrobe.

She watched him from the mirror as she finished fiddling around with her make-up. He looked heart-stoppingly gorgeous in that dark suit which emphasised the blackness of his hair and eyes. She wondered what Alice would say when she saw his name on the guest list. She wondered how he would fit in with all her work colleagues. But her heart was suddenly ridiculously light. He was coming, wasn't he? How could they fail to love him, as she loved him?

She had just slithered her dress over her head, when his words whispered through the air and startled her.

'You're not wearing that?'

She felt the clench of her heart, but she turned round to face him, a sanguine expression on her face. She smoothed her fingers down over the fine gold mesh and smiled. 'I am. Do you like it?'

'No.'

'Well, that's a pity. It's made by one of London's top designers, so it's eminently suitable for tonight's party.'

'It may be, but it is also much too short. You're practically showing your panties.'

The tone of his voice made her heart contract, but she was determined not to back down. She'd thought that they were over all this.

'Don't exaggerate, Suleiman—and please don't come over all heavy on me. The dress is a fashionable length and I'm wearing it. End of story.'

Their eyes met and she became aware of the silent war being waged between them and she tried to see it from his point of view. In Suleiman's world, a woman going out in public wearing a dress this short was sending out a very definite message.

'Look, I know it's the way you've been brought up,' she said. 'But you've really got to lose this idea that women are either saints or scrubbers. I'm wearing gold tights and long boots with it. The boots you bought me in Paris, actually—'

'And I bought those for you to wear in the bedroom.'

'Yes. Well, it may have missed your notice—' she lifted up her leg to reveal the sole of the boot '—but they have real heels made for walking. They weren't designed just for the bedroom! So are you going to lighten up and enjoy the evening?' Her gold bangles jangling, she walked over to him, placing one hand on his shoulder as she tilted her head to one side. 'Are you?'

There was a moment while their eyes fought another silent, clashing battle before Suleiman gave a low growl which was almost a laugh. 'No other woman would dare speak to me the way that you do, Sara.'

'That's why you love me, isn't it?'

'Maybe.' He slid his hand possessively around her waist. 'Come on. Let's go.'

CHAPTER TEN

MOODILY, SULEIMAN GLANCED around the vast art gallery. The cavernous space and endlessly high ceilings made him think that this might have been a warehouse in a former life, though the place certainly bore no resemblance to its humbler origins.

On white walls hung vast canvases sporting naïve splashes of colour which a five-year-old child could have achieved—all bearing price tags far beyond the reach of most ordinary mortals. Stick-thin women and geeky-looking men in glasses stood gazing up at them in rapt concentration, while waitresses dressed like extravagant birds offered trays of exotically coloured cocktails.

He still couldn't believe he was here. He couldn't believe that Sara had brought him here to look at these dull paintings and meet dull people, when she could have been in bed with him instead. He had been cooking her a meal. Didn't she realise that he'd never cooked for a woman before? But instead of switching off her phone and treating him with a little gratitude, she had brought him to this pretentious place. Had given him a plastic glass of very mediocre wine and then had disappeared to greet someone with one of those ridiculous air-kisses he so despised.

She needed to work, she had told him. Just as it seemed she always needed to work. She never stopped. It was as if she couldn't bear to get off the treadmill she'd leapt back on with such enthusiasm when they'd returned from Paris.

He watched her cross the room. The shimmer of her golden dress caressed her body as she moved, while the sinful blonde hair streamed over her shoulders in a silken cascade. Men were watching her, as they had been watching from the moment they'd arrived—even the geeky ones, who didn't particularly look as if they were into women. He wondered if she was aware of that. Was that why she had worn that skimpy little dress—to draw attention to her beauty? Was that what made her walk with such a seductive sway, or was that simply a consequence of wearing those indecently sexy boots?

Why had he bought her those damned boots?

She had stopped to talk to someone and her head was tilted upwards as she listened to what he was saying to her—a tall man with cold grey eyes and a chiselled face. They seemed to be having some kind of animated discussion. They acted as if they knew each other well and Suleiman's eyes narrowed. Who was he? He smiled with polite dismissal at the woman who had attached herself to his side like glue, and walked across the gallery until he had reached them.

Sara looked up as he approached and he noticed that

her cheeks had gone very pink. Had her male companion made her blush? he wondered. He felt the twist of something unfamiliar in his gut. Something dark and nebulous.

'Oh, Suleiman.' She smiled. 'There you are.'

'Here I am.' He looked at the man who stood beside her, with a questioning expression. 'Hello.'

He saw the way Sara's teeth had begun to dig into her bottom lip. Was she nervous, he wondered—and if so, why?

'I'd like to introduce you to my boss,' she was saying. 'This is Gabe Steel and he owns the best and biggest advertising agency in London. Gabe—this is Suleiman Abd al-Aziz and I've known...' She began to blush. 'Well, I've known Suleiman ever since I was a little girl.'

There was a split second as the two men eyed one another before briefly shaking hands and Suleiman found his fingers grasped with a bone-crushing strength which equalled his own. So this was her boss. The tycoon he had heard so much about and the man who had lent her his cottage at Christmas. A man with cold grey eyes and the kind of presence which was attracting almost as much attention from the women in the room as Suleiman himself.

One thought jarred uncomfortably in his head.

Why *had* he lent her his cottage?

'Good to meet you, Suleiman,' said Gabe. 'So tell me, was she a good little girl—or was she very naughty?'

Suleiman froze. He tried telling himself that this

was the normal, jokey kind of statement which existed among work colleagues in the west—but his heart was stubbornly refusing to listen to reason. Instead, his years of conditioning, which had resulted in a very rigid way of thinking, now demanded to be heard. Instead of joining in with the banter, he found himself thinking that this man Steel—no matter how exalted his position—was speaking most impertinently about the Princess of Dhi'ban.

Unless…

Suleiman's heart began to hammer painfully against his ribcage. Unless the relationship went deeper than that of mere workmates. He swallowed. Was it possible that Gabe Steel was the other man she had slept with— the man who had taken her virginity? Hadn't she told him on Christmas Eve that it was Gabe Steel's cottage and that she was *waiting for her lover*?

Had Gabe Steel been her lover?

For a moment he was so overcome by a sweep of jealousy so powerful that he couldn't speak, and when he did his words felt like little splinters of metal being expelled from his mouth.

'I don't think that the princess would wish me to divulge secrets from her past,' he said repressively.

'No, of course not.' Gabe looked startled, before flashing him an easy smile. 'So tell me, what do you think of the paintings?'

'You want my honest opinion?' Suleiman questioned.

'Suleiman's not a great connoisseur of art,' put in Sara hastily, before shooting him a furious look. She put her hand on his arm and pressed it—the sharp dig undeniably warning him not to elaborate. 'Are you, darling?'

Suleiman felt a cold fury begin to rise within him. She was speaking to him as if he were some tame little lapdog she had brought along with her. But he could see that causing a scene here would serve no purpose, except to delay their departure and ensure her fury. Clearly she danced obediently to this man Steel's tune—and when they got home he would do her the favour of pointing it out.

So he merely gave a bland smile as he reached out and drew her against him, a proprietorial thumb moving very deliberately over her ribcage. He felt her shiver beneath his touch and he allowed himself a small smile of satisfaction as he looked at her boss.

'Sara's right, of course. I have never been able to understand the penchant for spending vast sums of money on modern art. Call me old-fashioned—but I prefer something which doesn't look as if a cat has regurgitated its supper all over the canvas.'

'Oh, I think we could certainly call you old-fashioned, Suleiman,' said Sara in a high, bright voice.

'But I can see that your campaign has been successful,' conceded Suleiman, forcing a smile. 'Judging by the amount of people here tonight.'

'Yes, we're very pleased with the turnout,' said Gabe. 'Much of which is down to the talent of your girlfriend, of course. It was her artwork which made people sit up and start taking notice.' He smiled. 'Sara's one of the best creatives I have.'

'I'm sure she is. I just hope you have a good replacement ready to step in to fill her shoes,' said Suleiman.

He could see the look of surprise on Gabe Steel's face and the sudden draining of colour from Sara's.

'Something you're not telling me?' questioned Gabe lightly.

'Nothing that I know of,' she answered as her boss gave a brief nod of his head and walked across the art gallery to talk to a woman on the other side of the room.

'Shall we go home?' questioned Suleiman.

'I think we'd better,' said Sara quietly. 'Before I smash one of those very expensive "regurgitated cat supper" canvases over your arrogant head.'

'Are you saying you'd like one of those hanging in your living room?'

'I do happen to like some of them, yes, but I'm not going to have a conversation about the artwork.'

Suleiman kept his hand firmly on her waist as he steered her towards the cloakroom, so that she could collect her wrap.

She didn't speak until they were outside and neither did he, but just before he opened the door of the waiting cab he leaned into her, breathing in her scent of jasmine and patchouli oil. 'Just what is your relationship with Steel?'

'Don't,' she snapped back. 'Don't you dare say another word, until we're back at my apartment.' She began speaking to him in Qurhahian then, her heated words coming out in a furious tirade. 'I don't want

the cab driver thinking I'm out with some kind of *Neanderthal*!'

She made no attempt to hide her anger all the way through the constant stop-starting of traffic lights but Suleiman felt nothing but the slow build of sexual hunger in response. The stubborn profile she presented made him want her. Her defiantly tilted chin made him want her even more. He felt the hardening at his groin. He would subdue her fire in the most satisfying way. Subdue her so completely and utterly that she wouldn't ever defy him again. She wouldn't want to...

Feeling more frustrated than he could ever remember, he watched as the orange, green and red of the traffic lights flickered over her face. The flickering kaleidoscope of colour and the sparkle of her golden dress only added to her beauty.

If it had been any other woman, he would have just pulled her in his arms and kissed her. Maybe even brought her to gasping orgasm on the back seat of the cab. But this was not any other woman. It was Sara. Fiery and beautiful Princess Sara. Stubborn and sensual Sara.

The elevator ride up to her apartment was torture. The heat at his groin almost too painful to endure. All he could see was the glimmer of gold as her dress highlighted every curve of her magnificent body, but her shoulders were stiff with tension and her face was still furious.

It seemed to take for ever before the lift pinged to a halt and they were back in her apartment again. The front door had barely closed behind them before she turned on him. 'How *dare* you behave like that?'

'Like what?'

'Coming over all possessive and squaring up to my boss like that!'

'So why the sudden defence of Steel, Sara? Was he your lover? The man to whom you lost your innocence?'

'Oh!' Frustratedly, she stared at him for a piercing moment before turning her back and marching into the sitting room, just the way she'd done on Christmas Eve at the cottage. And just like then, he followed her—mesmerised by the shimmering sway of her bottom, until she turned round to glare at him again.

The violet flash in her eyes warned him not to continue with his line of questioning, but Suleiman found he was in the grip of an emotion far bigger than reason. *'Was* he?' he demanded hotly. 'Is that why he lent you his cottage? Why you were so keen to get to the party tonight?'

She shook her head. 'You just don't *get* it, do you? You don't seem to realise that I've been living in England for all these years and I'm just not used to men behaving like this. It's *primitive.* And it's inappropriate.'

'I don't think it's inappropriate,' he ground out. 'You told me that night that you were waiting for your lover and that it was Steel's cottage. Then I discovered that you were not a virgin and so I put two and two together—'

'And came up with a number which seems to have

reached triple figures!' she flared, before taking a deep breath as if she was trying to get her own feelings under control. 'Look, I shouldn't have said that about Gabe that night. I was trying to make you angry—and it seems that I have far exceeded my own expectations. I was hurling out stuff and hoping to get a reaction. But I said all that before we became...involved. For the record, Gabe has never been my lover. But even if he had...*even if he had*...that does not give you the right to just march up to him like that in public and start playing the jealousy card. I just don't get it.'

'What don't you get?' he demanded. 'That a man should feel possessive about the woman he loves? Isn't that a mark of the way he feels about her?'

She shook her head. 'It's got nothing to do with the way he feels about her—it's more a mark of wanting to *own* her! Before you became Mr Oil Baron, you travelled for years on Murat's behalf. Are you trying to tell me that this is the way you behaved whenever you met with some diplomat or politician whose ideas you didn't happen to agree with? Going in with all guns blazing?'

His eyes narrowed. 'On the contrary. One of the reasons I excel at card games is because I have the ability to conceal what I'm thinking.'

Slowly, she nodded her head 'So what happened tonight?'

'You did,' he said. 'You happened.'

'You mean it's something I did?'

He shook his head. 'I'm having trouble working it out for myself. I've never *felt* this way about a woman before, and sometimes it scares the hell out of me. I've never wanted a woman in the way I want you, Sara.'

'But wanting me doesn't give you permission to behave like that towards Gabe. It doesn't give you the right to start treating me like a *thing*. Like a valuable painting or some vase that you own, which nobody else is allowed to look at, because it's *all yours*. I don't want that.'

For a moment there was silence as he looked at her.

'Then just what *do* you want, Sara?' he questioned. 'Because you don't seem to want a normal relationship. Not from where I'm standing.'

'That's funny. A normal relationship? I don't think you'd recognise one if you tripped over it in the street!' she said. 'And how could you? You're possessive and demanding and insanely jealous.'

'And you don't think that you might have fed my instinct to be jealous?'

'I've already explained about Gabe.'

'I'm not talking about Gabe! I'm talking about the fact that ever since I've moved in here, you seem to be pushing me away. It's like you've surrounded yourself with a glass wall and I just can't get through to you.'

She felt the fear licking at the edges of her skin. Was that true—or did Suleiman just want to make her completely his, and to stamp out all her natural fire and independence?

She couldn't risk it.

'Oh, what's the point?' she said tiredly. 'There is no point. We've shone the light on what we've got and seen all the gaping great cracks.'

'I think you've made up your mind that it isn't going to work,' he said. 'And maybe that's the way it has to be. But since you've had your say, then let me have mine. And yes, I hold my hands up to all the charges you've just levelled at me. Yes, I've been "possessive and demanding and insanely jealous". I'm not proud of the way I behaved earlier and I'm sorry. It's been bubbling away for a while now and tonight it just seemed to spill over. But I wonder if you've stopped for a minute to ask yourself why?'

'Because you're still living in the Dark Ages? A typical desert male who will never change?'

He shook his head. 'Let me tell you something else, Sara—that I may have failed to live up to your ideal of the ideal lover tonight, but I've sure as hell tried in other ways.'

'How?' She felt stupid standing there in her golden dress with her bangles dangling from her limp wrist. Like a butterfly which had been speared by a pin. 'How have you tried?'

'*How?* For a start, I have relocated into your poky London apartment—'

'It is *not* poky!'

'Oh, believe me,' he said grimly, 'it is. I've been trying to run a global business from the second bedroom and all I get from you is complaints about the phone ringing at odd hours.'

'Is that *all* you get from me, Suleiman?'

He heard the unconsciously sultry note which had entered her voice and wondered if their angry words had scared her. And turned her on. Because didn't women like to push a man to the brink—even though sometimes they didn't like what happened when they got there?

'No,' he said. 'I get a lot of good stuff, too. The best stuff ever, if you must know—but what we have is not sustainable.'

'Not *sustainable*?'

He hardened his heart against the sudden darkening of her eyes and, even though he wanted to cross the room and pull her into his arms, he stood his ground. 'You think I'm content to continue to be treated as some kind of mild irrelevance, while your job dominates everything?'

'I told you that I needed to work.'

'And I accepted that. I just hadn't realised that you would be living at the office, virtually 24/7—as if you had to prove yourself. I don't know if it was to me, or to your boss—to reassure him that you weren't going to take off again. Or to show me that you're an independent woman in your own right. But whatever it is—you aren't facing up to the truth behind your actions.'

'And you are, right?'

'Maybe I am. And I'll tell you what you seem so determined to ignore, if that's what you want, Sara. Or even if it's not what you want. Because I think you need to hear it.'

'Oh, do you?' She walked over to one of the squashy pink velvet sofas and sat down on it, leaning back with her arms crossed over her chest and a defiant expression on her face. 'Go on, then. I can hardly wait.'

His eyes narrowed, because he could hear the vulnerability she was trying so hard to hide. But he needed to say this. No matter what the consequences. 'I get it that you grew up in an unhappy home and that your mother felt trapped. But you are not your mother. Your circumstances are completely different.'

'Not that different,' she whispered. 'Not when you treated me like that tonight. Like your possession.'

'I've held up my hands for that. I've said sorry. I would tell you truthfully that I would never behave in that way again, but it's too late.'

Her arms fell to her side. 'What do you mean, too late?'

'For us. I've tried to change and to adapt to being with you. I may not have instantly succeeded, but at least I gave it a go. But not you. You've stayed locked inside your own fear. You're scared, Sara. You're scared of who you really are. That's what made you run away from Dhi'ban. That's why you let your job consume you.'

'My father gave me permission to go away to boarding school—I didn't *run away*.'

'But you never go back, do you?'

'Because my life is here.'

'I know it is. But you have family. Your only family, in fact. When did you last see your brother? I heard that you were at his wedding celebrations for less than twenty-four hours.'

Briefly she wondered how he knew something like that. Had he been *spying* on her? 'I couldn't stay for long…I was in the middle of an important job.'

'Sure you were. Just like you always are. But you have vacations like other people, don't you, Sara? Couldn't you have gone over to see him from time to time? Didn't you ever think that being a king can be a lonely job? Hasn't his wife had a baby? Have you even *seen* your niece?'

'I sent them a gift when she was born,' she said defensively, and saw his mouth harden with an expression which suddenly made her feel very uncomfortable.

'You might want to reject your past,' he grated. 'But you can't deny the effect it's had on you. You may hate some things about desert life—but half of you *is* of the desert. Hide from that and you're hiding from yourself—and that's a scary place to be. I know that. You were one of the reasons I knew I could no longer work for Murat, but what happened between us that night made me re-examine my life. I realised that I couldn't continue playing a subordinate role out of some lingering sense of gratitude to a man who had plucked me from poverty.' He looked at her. 'But that's all irrelevant now. I need to pack.'

Her head jerked up as if she were a puppet and somebody had just given the string a particularly violent tug. 'Pack? What for?' She could hear the rising note of panic in her voice. 'What are you packing for?'

'I'm going.' His voice was almost gentle. 'It's over, Sara. We've had good times and bad times, but it's over. I recognise that and sooner or later you will, too. And I don't want to destroy all the good memories by continuing to slug it out, so I'm leaving now.'

She was swallowing convulsively. 'But it's late.'

'I know it is.'

'You could... Couldn't you stay tonight and go in the morning?'

'I can't do that, Sara.'

'No.' She shrugged as if it didn't matter. As if she didn't care. 'No, I guess you can't.'

Her lips were trembling as she watched him turn round and walk from the sitting room. She could hear the sounds he made as he clattered around in the bathroom, presumably clearing away that lethal-looking razor he always used. A terrible sense of sadness—and an even greater sense of failure—washed over her as he appeared in the doorway, carrying his leather overnight bag.

'I'll collect the rest of my stuff tomorrow, while you're at work.'

She stood up. Her legs were unsteady. She wanted to run over to him and tell him to stop. That it had all been a horrible mistake. Like a bad dream which you woke from and discovered that none of it had been real. But this *was* real. Real and very painful.

She wasn't going to be that red-eyed woman clinging onto his leg as he walked out of the door, she reminded herself. *Was she?* And surely they could say goodbye properly. A lifetime of friendship didn't have to end like *this*.

'A last kiss?' she said lightly, sounding like some vacuous socialite he'd just met at a cocktail party.

His mouth hardened. He looked...*appalled*. As if

she had just suggested holding an all-night rave on someone's grave.

'I don't think so,' he said grimly, before turning to slam his way out of her apartment—leaving only a terrible echoing emptiness behind.

CHAPTER ELEVEN

THE APARTMENT FELT bare without him.

Her life felt bare without him.

Sara felt as if she'd woken up on a different planet.

It reminded her of when she'd arrived at her boarding school in England, at the impressionable age of twelve. It had been a bitter September day, and the contrast to the hot desert country she'd left behind couldn't have been more different. She remembered shivering as the leaves began to be ripped from the trees by the wind, and she'd had to get used to the unspeakably stodgy food and cold, dark mornings. And even though she had known that here in England lay the future she had wanted—it had still felt like being on an alien planet for a while.

But that was nothing to the way she felt now that Suleiman had gone.

Hadn't she thought—prayed—that he hadn't meant it? That he would have cooled off by morning. That he would come back and they could make up. She could say sorry, as he had done. They could learn from their mistakes, and work out what they both wanted from their lives and walk forward into the future together.

He didn't come back.

She watched the clock. She checked her phone. She waited in.

And even though her pride tried to stop her— eventually she dialled his number. She was clutching a golden pen she'd found on the floor of the second bedroom—the only reminder that Suleiman had ever used the room as an office. He had loved this pen and would miss it, she convinced herself, even though she knew he had a dozen other pens he could use.

But he didn't pick up. The phone rang through to a brisk-sounding male assistant, who told her that Suleiman was travelling. In as casual a tone as she could manage, she found herself asking where—only to suffer the humiliation of the assistant telling her that security issues meant that he would rather not say.

Where was he travelling to? Sara wondered—as she put the phone down with a trembling hand. Had he gone back to Paris? Was he lying in that penthouse suite with another blonde climbing all over him wearing kinky boots and tiny knickers?

With a shaking hand she put the gold pen down carefully on the desk and then she forced herself to dress and went into the office.

But for the first time in her life, she couldn't concentrate on work.

Alice asked her several questions, which she had to repeat because Sara wasn't paying attention. Then she spilt her coffee over a drawing she'd been working on and completely ruined it. The days seemed to rush past her in a dark stream of heartache. Her thoughts wouldn't focus. She couldn't seem to allocate her time into anything resembling *order*. Everything seemed a mess.

At the end of the week, Gabe called her into the office and asked her to sit down and she could see from his face that he wasn't happy.

'What's wrong?' he questioned bluntly.

'Nothing's wrong.'

'Sara,' he said. 'If you can't do your job properly, then you really shouldn't come to work.'

She swallowed. 'That bad, huh?'

He shrugged. 'Do you want to talk about it?'

Miserably, she shook her head. Gabe was a good boss in many ways but she knew what they said about him—steely by name and steely by nature. 'Not really.'

'Look, take a week off,' he said. 'And for God's sake, sort it out.'

She nodded, thinking that men really *were* very different from women. It was all so black and white to them. What if it couldn't be sorted out? What if Suleiman had gone from her life for good?

She left the building and walked out into the fresh air, where a gust of wind seemed to blow right through her. She hugged her sheepskin coat closer and began to walk, thinking about the things Suleiman had said to her.

Thoughts she'd been trying to block out were now given free rein as she examined them. *Had* she run away from her old life and tried to deny it? Pretended that part of her didn't exist?

Yes, she had.

Had she behaved thoughtlessly, neglecting the only family she had? Rushing away from the wedding celebrations and not even bothering to get on a plane to go and see her new niece?

She closed her eyes.

Yes, again.

She'd thought of herself as so independent and mature, and yet the first thing she had done was to lift up the phone to Suleiman. What had she been planning to say to him? Start whining that she missed him and wanted him to come back to make her feel better?

That wasn't independence, was it? That was more like co-dependence. And you couldn't rely on somebody else to make you feel better about yourself.

She needed to face up to the stuff she'd locked away for so long. She'd been so busy playing the part of Sara Williams who had integrated so well into English life and making sure she fitted in that she had forgotten the other Sara.

The desert princess. The sister. The auntie.

And that other Sara was just as important.

A lump came into her throat as she lifted her hand to hail a cab and during the drive to her apartment she started making plans to try to put it right.

She managed to get a flight out to Dhi'ban later that evening. It meant she would have a two-hour stopover in Qurhah, but she could cope with that. Oddly enough, she wasn't tempted to ask her brother to send a plane to Qurhah to collect her—and she would sooner walk bare-footed across the desert than ask Suleiman to come to her aid.

She spent the intervening hours shopping and packing and then she dressed as conservatively and as unobtrusively as possible, because she didn't want anyone getting wind of her spontaneous visit.

The journey was long and tiring and she blinked with surprise when eventually she arrived at Dhi'ban's main airport, because she hardly recognised it. The terminal buildings had been extended and were now gleaming and modern. There were loads of shops selling cosmetics and beautiful Dhi'banese jewellery and clothes. And there…

She looked up to see a portrait of her brother, the King, and she thought how stern he looked. Sterner than she'd ever seen him, wearing the crown that her father had worn.

Inevitably, she was recognised as she went through Customs, but she waved aside the troubled protestations of the officials, telling them that she had no desire for a red carpet.

'I didn't want any kind of fuss or reception,' she said, smiling as she held up the large pink parcel she had purchased at Qurhah's airport. 'I want this to be a surprise. For my niece, the princess Ayesha.'

The palm-fringed road was reassuringly familiar and when she saw her childhood home appear in the distance, with the morning light bouncing off the white marble, she felt her heart twist with a mixture of pleasure and pain.

She'd never seen the guards outside the main gates look more surprised than when she stepped from the airport cab into the bright sunshine. But today she wasn't impatient when they bowed deeply. Today she recognised that they were just doing their job. They respected her position as Princess—and maybe it was about time that she started respecting it, too.

She walked through the grounds and into the palace. Her watch told her that it was almost two o'clock and she wondered if her brother was working. She realised that she didn't know anything about his life and she barely knew Ella, his wife.

But before she could decide what to do next, there was Haroun walking towards her. His features—a stronger, more masculine version of her own—were initially perplexed and then he broke into a wide smile as he held out his arms.

'Is it really you, Sara?'

'It really is me,' she whispered, glad that he chose that moment to gather her in his arms in a most un-Kingly bear-hug, which meant that she had time to blink away her tears and compose herself.

Within the hour she was sitting with Haroun and his wife Ella and begging their forgiveness. She told them she felt guilty about her absence, but if they were prepared to forgive her—she would like to be part of their lives. And could she please see her niece?

The royal couple looked at one another and smiled with deep satisfaction, before Ella hugged her tightly and said Ayesha was sleeping, and that Sara could see her once they had taken tea.

The three of them sat in the scented bower of the rose garden and drank mint tea. She started to tell them about the Sultan, but of course Haroun knew about the cancelled wedding, because the politicians and diplomats from the two countries were working on a new alliance.

'So you've *seen* Murat?' she asked cautiously.

'I have.'

'And did he...did he seem upset?'

'Not unless your idea of upset is being photographed with a stunning woman,' laughed Haroun.

It was only after gentle prompting that she was persuaded to tell them about Suleiman and how much she loved him. Her voice was shaky as she said it, because she'd realised that the truth was something she couldn't keep running from either.

'But it's over,' she said.

Ella looked at Haroun, and frowned. 'You *like* Suleiman, don't you, darling?'

'I don't like him when I'm playing backgammon,' Haroun growled.

Sara was shown to her old room and there, set between the two gold-framed portraits of her late mother and father, was a book about horses, which Suleiman had bought for her twelfth birthday, just before she'd left for England.

For the brave and fearless Sara, he had written. *Your friend, Suleiman. Always.*

And that was when the sobs began to erupt from her throat, because she had been none of those things, had she? She had not been brave and fearless—she had been a coward who had run away and hidden and neglected her family. She hadn't lived up to Suleiman's expectations of her. She hadn't been a real friend. She hadn't fulfilled her potential in so many ways.

She bathed and changed and dried her eyes and Ella knocked on the door, to take her to the nursery. And that was poignant, too. Shielded from the light by swathed swags of softest tulle lay a sleeping baby in the large, rocking cot she had slept in herself. For a moment Sara touched the side and felt it sway, watching as Ella lifted out the sleepy infant.

Ayesha was soft and smiling, with a mop of silken curls and a pair of deep violet eyes. Sara felt her heart fill with love as she touched her fingertip to the baby's plump and rosy cheek.

'Oh, she's beautiful,' she said. 'How old is she now?'

'Nine months,' said Ella. 'I know. Time flies and all that. And by the way—they say she looks just like you.'

'Do they?'

Ella smiled. 'Check out your baby photos if you don't believe me.'

Sara stared into the baby's eyes and felt the sharp twist of pain. Was it normal to feel wistful for what might have been, but now never would? To imagine what kind of baby she and Suleiman might have produced?

'I wonder if she'd come to me,' she said, pulling a smiley face at the baby as she held out her arms.

But Ayesha wriggled and turned her face away and started to cry.

'Don't worry,' said Ella. 'She'll get used to you.'

It took four days before Ayesha would consent to have her auntie hold her, but once she had—she seemed reluctant to ever let her go. Sara wondered if the baby instinctively guessed how badly she needed the cuddles. Or maybe there was some kind of inbuilt recognition—the primitive bond of shared blood.

She fitted in with Haroun and Ella's routine, and began to relax as she reacquainted herself with Dhi'ban and life at court. She went riding with her brother. She helped Ella with the baby and quickly grew to love her sister-in-law.

One afternoon the two women were wheeling the pram through the palace gardens, their heads covered with shady hats. The week off work which Gabe had given her was almost up and Sara knew that she needed to give some serious thought to her future.

She just hadn't decided what she wanted that future to be.

'Shall we go back now?' questioned Ella, her soft voice breaking into Sara's thoughts.

'Yes, let's.'

Along the scented paths they walked, back towards the palace, but as they grew closer Sara saw a dark figure silhouetted against the white marble building. For a moment her eyes widened, until she forced her troubled mind to listen to reason. *Please stop this,* she prayed silently. *Stop conjuring up hallucinations which make me think I can actually see him.*

She ran her hand across her eyelids, but when she opened them again he was still there and her steps faltered.

'Is something wrong?'

Did Ella's voice contain suppressed laughter—or was she imagining *that*, too?

'For a minute then, I thought I saw Suleiman.'

'Well, that's because you did,' said Ella gently. 'He's here. Suleiman's here.'

The ground seemed suddenly to shift beneath Sara's feet—the way it did when you stepped onto a large ship which looked motionless. She was aware of the rush of blood to her ears and the pounding of her heart in her chest. Questions streamed into her mind but her lips seemed too dry to do anything other than stumble out one bewildered word. 'How?'

But Ella was walking away, wheeling the pram towards one of the side entrances, and Sara was left standing there, feeling exposed and scared and impossibly vulnerable. Now her legs felt heavy. As if her feet had suddenly turned to stone and it was going to be impossible for her to walk. But she *had* to walk. Independent women walked. They didn't stumble—weak-kneed and hopeless—because the man they dreamed of had just appeared, like a blazing dark comet which had fallen to earth.

He didn't move as she went towards him and it was impossible to read the expression on his dark face. Even as she grew closer she still couldn't tell what he was thinking. But hadn't he told her himself that he was famous at the card table for being able to keep a poker-straight face?

She was trying to quell the hope which had risen up inside her—because dashed hopes were surely worse than no hope at all. But she couldn't keep her voice steady as she stood before him, and the pain of wanting to hold him again was almost physical.

'Suleiman,' she said and her voice sounded croaky and unsure. 'What are you doing here?'

'I've come to speak to your brother about the possibility of drilling for oil in Dhi'ban.'

Her heart plummeted. 'Are you being serious?'

He looked at her, an expression of exasperation on his face. 'Of course I'm not being serious. Why do you *think* I might be here, Sara?'

'I don't *know*!'

She was shaking her head and, for the first time, Suleiman saw that she had changed—even if for a moment he couldn't quite work out what that change was. Her skin was a little paler than usual and her lips looked as if they had been bitten into—but beneath all that he could see something else. Something which had been missing for a long time. He swallowed down the sudden lump in his throat as he realised that something was peace. That there was a new strength and resolution which shone out from her shadowed eyes as she looked at him.

And now he began to have doubts of his own. Had Sara found true contentment—*without* him? For a moment he acknowledged that his motives for being here today were entirely selfish. What if she would be better off without him? Had he stopped to consider *that*? Was her need for independence such that she considered a man like him to be an impediment?

His heart turning over with love and pain, he looked

into her beautiful face and suddenly he didn't care. He knew there were no guarantees in this life, but that didn't mean you shouldn't strike out for the things which really mattered. Let Sara tell him that she didn't want him if that was what she truly believed—but let her be in no doubt about his feelings for her.

'I think you do know,' he said softly. 'I'm here because I love you and I can't seem to stop loving you.'

'Did you try?' she questioned, her voice full of pain. 'Is that why you walked away? Why you left my life so utterly when you walked out of my apartment?'

There was a silence for a moment, broken only by the sound of a bird calling from high up in one of the trees. 'I couldn't stay when you were like that,' he told her truthfully. 'When you were too scared to let go and be the woman you really wanted to be. You were pushing me away, Sara—and I couldn't stand that. I knew you needed to come home before you could think about making any kind of home of your own.' He smiled. 'Then I heard on the desert grapevine that you'd come back to Dhi'ban. And I thought that was probably the best thing I'd heard in a long time.'

She turned big violet eyes up at him. 'Did you?'

'Mmm.' He wanted to go to her. To cup her chin in the palm of his hand and hold it safe. To run the edge of his thumb over the tremble of her lips. But he needed her to hear these words before he could touch her again. He owed her his honesty.

'As for the answer to your question. I'm here because you make me feel stuff—stuff I've spent a lifetime trying not to feel.'

'What kind of stuff?'

'Love.'

'Oh. You *think* you love me?' she questioned, echoing the words he had used in Paris.

'No.' His voice was quiet. 'I *love* you—without qualification. I love you fully, completely, utterly and for ever. I'm here because although I'm perfectly capable of living without you, I don't want to. No. That's not entirely true. If you want the truth, I can't bear the thought of living without you, Sara. Because without you I am only half the man I'm capable of being and I want to be whole.'

There was silence for a moment. She lowered her gaze, as if she had found something of immense interest on the gravelled palace forecourt. For a moment he wondered if she was plucking up the courage to tell him that his journey here had been wasted, but when she lifted her face again, Suleiman could see the shimmer of tears in her violet eyes.

'And without you I'm only half the woman I'm capable of being,' she said shakily. 'You've made me whole again, too. You've made me realise that only by facing our biggest fears can we overcome them. You've made me realise that independence is a good thing—but it can never be at the expense of love. Nothing can. Because love is the most important thing of all. And you are the most important thing of all, Suleiman—someone so precious who I thought I'd lost through my own stupidity.'

'Sara,' he said and the word was distorted by the shudder of his breath. 'Sweet Sara. My only love.'

And that was all it took. A declaration torn from somewhere deep inside him. A declaration she returned over and over again in between their frantic kisses, although Suleiman first took the precaution of walking her further into the gardens, away from the natural interest of the servants' eyes.

By the time they returned to the palace—where Ella and Haroun had perceptively put a bottle of champagne on ice—Sara was wearing an enormous emerald engagement ring.

And she couldn't seem to stop smiling.

EPILOGUE

'YOU DO REALISE,' said Sara as she removed her filmy tulle veil and placed it next to the emerald and diamond tiara, which her sister-in-law had lent her, 'that I'm not going to be a traditional desert wife.'

'Shouldn't you have mentioned this *before* we got married?' murmured Suleiman. He was lying naked waiting for his bride to join him on her old childhood bed, and had decided that there was something gloriously decadent about that.

'I did.' She stepped out of her ivory lace gown and hung it over the back of the chair, revelling in the look in his eyes as he ran his gaze over her bridal lingerie. 'Just as long as you know that I meant it.'

'And I meant it when I said that I didn't expect you to be. Just as I did when I said that I will not be a traditional desert husband. I will not try to possess you, Sara—not ever again. I will give you all the freedom you need.'

She gave a happy sigh as she smiled at him. Wasn't it a strange thing that when somebody gave you freedom, it meant you no longer wanted it quite so much?

Suleiman had told her that of course she could carry on working for Gabe—just as long as they came to some compromise over her long hours. The crazy thing was that she no longer wanted to work there—or, at least, not as she'd done before. She had loved her job, but it was part of her past and part of her life as a single woman. She had a different life now and different opportunities. Which was why she had agreed to carry on working for the Steel organisation on a freelance basis. That way, she could travel with her husband and everyone was happy.

She gave a contented sigh. Their wedding had been the best wedding she'd ever been to—although Suleiman told her she was biased. Alice from the office had been invited—and her expression as she'd been shown around the Dhi'ban palace had been priceless. Gabe had been there too—and Sara thought that even her cynical boss had enjoyed all the ancient ritual and ceremony which accompanied the joining of her hand to Suleiman's.

The best bit had been the Sultan's surprise appearance, because it signified that he had forgiven Suleiman—and her—for so radically changing the course of desert history.

'Murat seemed to get on well with Gabe, don't you think?' she questioned as she slid her diamond bracelet onto the dressing table, where it lay coiled like a glittery snake. 'What do you suppose they were talking about?'

'Right now I don't care,' Suleiman murmured.

'About anything other than kissing you again. It seems like an eternity since I had you in my bed.'

'It's almost a week since you had me in your bed— palace protocol being what it is,' she agreed. 'But less than eight hours since you *had* me. *In* the stables, no less—on the eve of my wedding. And I wasn't allowed to make a sound.'

'That was part of the thrill,' he drawled, watching as she kicked off her high-heeled shoes. 'Not very much keeps you quiet, but it seems that at last I've found something which does. Which means that we are going to be indulging in lots of illicit sex in the future, my darling wife.'

She walked over to the bed to join him, still wearing her panties, her bra and her white lace suspender belt and stockings. It felt warm in his embrace, and safe. So very safe.

They were going to honeymoon in Samahan and she was going to learn all about the land of Suleiman's birth. Afterwards, they would decide where they wanted to make their main base.

'It can be anywhere,' he had promised her. 'Anywhere at all.'

She closed her eyes as he tightened his arms around her, because where they lived didn't matter.

This was home.

* * * * *

Mills & Boon® Hardback
December 2013

ROMANCE

Defiant in the Desert	Sharon Kendrick
Not Just the Boss's Plaything	Caitlin Crews
Rumours on the Red Carpet	Carole Mortimer
The Change in Di Navarra's Plan	Lynn Raye Harris
The Prince She Never Knew	Kate Hewitt
His Ultimate Prize	Maya Blake
More than a Convenient Marriage?	Dani Collins
A Hunger for the Forbidden	Maisey Yates
The Reunion Lie	Lucy King
The Most Expensive Night of Her Life	Amy Andrews
Second Chance with Her Soldier	Barbara Hannay
Snowed in with the Billionaire	Caroline Anderson
Christmas at the Castle	Marion Lennox
Snowflakes and Silver Linings	Cara Colter
Beware of the Boss	Leah Ashton
Too Much of a Good Thing?	Joss Wood
After the Christmas Party...	Janice Lynn
Date with a Surgeon Prince	Meredith Webber

MEDICAL

From Venice with Love	Alison Roberts
Christmas with Her Ex	Fiona McArthur
Her Mistletoe Wish	Lucy Clark
Once Upon a Christmas Night...	Annie Claydon

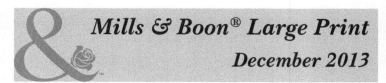

ROMANCE

The Billionaire's Trophy	Lynne Graham
Prince of Secrets	Lucy Monroe
A Royal Without Rules	Caitlin Crews
A Deal with Di Capua	Cathy Williams
Imprisoned by a Vow	Annie West
Duty at What Cost?	Michelle Conder
The Rings That Bind	Michelle Smart
A Marriage Made in Italy	Rebecca Winters
Miracle in Bellaroo Creek	Barbara Hannay
The Courage To Say Yes	Barbara Wallace
Last-Minute Bridesmaid	Nina Harrington

HISTORICAL

Not Just a Governess	Carole Mortimer
A Lady Dares	Bronwyn Scott
Bought for Revenge	Sarah Mallory
To Sin with a Viking	Michelle Willingham
The Black Sheep's Return	Elizabeth Beacon

MEDICAL

NYC Angels: Making the Surgeon Smile	Lynne Marshall
NYC Angels: An Explosive Reunion	Alison Roberts
The Secret in His Heart	Caroline Anderson
The ER's Newest Dad	Janice Lynn
One Night She Would Never Forget	Amy Andrews
When the Cameras Stop Rolling...	Connie Cox

Mills & Boon® Hardback
January 2014

ROMANCE

The Dimitrakos Proposition	Lynne Graham
His Temporary Mistress	Cathy Williams
A Man Without Mercy	Miranda Lee
The Flaw in His Diamond	Susan Stephens
Forged in the Desert Heat	Maisey Yates
The Tycoon's Delicious Distraction	Maggie Cox
A Deal with Benefits	Susanna Carr
The Most Expensive Lie of All	Michelle Conder
The Dance Off	Ally Blake
Confessions of a Bad Bridesmaid	Jennifer Rae
The Greek's Tiny Miracle	Rebecca Winters
The Man Behind the Mask	Barbara Wallace
English Girl in New York	Scarlet Wilson
The Final Falcon Says I Do	Lucy Gordon
Mr (Not Quite) Perfect	Jessica Hart
After the Party	Jackie Braun
Her Hard to Resist Husband	Tina Beckett
Mr Right All Along	Jennifer Taylor

MEDICAL

The Rebel Doc Who Stole Her Heart	Susan Carlisle
From Duty to Daddy	Sue MacKay
Changed by His Son's Smile	Robin Gianna
Her Miracle Twins	Margaret Barker

Mills & Boon® Large Print
January 2014

ROMANCE

HISTORICAL

MEDICAL

1213 GEN STD LP